About the author

Jean Ure was still at school when she had her first novel published. After finishing school she took on a variety of jobs to support herself while she continued to write: cook, floor-scrubber, translator, temp, trainee nurse, usherette and shop assistant. Then, after spending two years in Paris, she enrolled at the Webber-Douglas Academy of Drama where she trained as an actress.

Jean has written more than eighty books, and you can read about some of them on her website (www.jeanure.com). Jean is widely recognised as one of the most successful and popular authors in this country. "Writing," she says, "is the only proper job I've ever had!". Just Sixteen is Jean's second book for the Black Apple list. Her first was Love is Forever, a thought-provoking novel about relationships and prejudices.

Jean lives in a 300-year-old house in Croydon with her husband, seven dogs and four cats.

For Kait, who made me think.
And also for Nick Tucker, who
wrote an article which set the
whole thing off.

ORCHARD BOOKS
338 Euston Road, London NW1 3BH
Orchard Books Australia
Hachette Children's Books
Level 17/207 Kent Street, Sydney, NSW 2000

ISBN 978 1 84362 940 5

First published in 1999 by Orchard Books
This edition published in 2008
A paperback original

A CIP catalogue record for this book is available from the British Library.

1 3 5 7 9 10 9 7 5 3
Printed in Great Britain

Orchard Books is a division of Hachette Children's Books,
an Hachette Livre UK company

www.orchardbooks.co.uk

JEAN URE

Also by Jean Ure

Love is for Ever
Get a Life

and the Girlfriends series:

Pink Knickers Aren't Cool!
Girls Stick Together!
Girls Are Groovy!
Boys Are OK!

Chapter One

It's a funny thing about nicknames. They're supposed to mean that people are – well! Kind of fond of you. Like for instance there's this guy in our class called Barry Rainsford that everyone calls Bazza. I mean, they wouldn't do that if they didn't think he was good old Baz. They wouldn't do it if he were a scumbag or a nerd.

Then there's Ross McFadden. He's called Shorty on account of he's two metres tall. And this girl, Sue Tizzard, that everyone calls Tizz. And Dan Barnard, known as Barney.

What I'm saying is, if people don't like them, they wouldn't give them nicknames. Right? So you have a nickname, you probably ought to be pretty pleased about it. Except that I'm not. You want to know what my nickname is? Shall I tell you what my nickname is? My nickname is Ginny. Short for Virginia.

OK! So what's wrong with that? Nothing, really, I guess, except that I'm a bloke.

I'm here to tell you that it is no fun being called by a girl's name where you're not a girl. How it all started, it was way back in Year 7 when some joker discovered that *virgo* was the Latin for virgin. Virgo is my surname. *Unfortunately.* We were learning this crappy carol for the Christmas carol service and they had to go and write this one line in Latin. It nearly caused a riot. Sam's a virgin! Sammy Virgin! Tee-hee, har-har, ho-ho. Wot a larf!

I guess I didn't mind it so much then. I mean, we were only eleven years old, for heaven's sake. Eleven or twelve. Everyone's a virgin at eleven or twelve. Well, I have my doubts about Gemma Watkin, I reckon she started off in her cradle. But all the rest of us. We were green as grass.

Thing is, by the time we got to Year 11 it wasn't so funny any more. We were fifteen by now; going on sixteen. And they were still at it! Still calling me Virginia. Or Ginny. Or sometimes Gin. Gin was OK. I didn't get too aerated about Gin. Gin, whisky, vodka. No problem. It was Virginia that really got me. I mean, what did all those little kids from Year 7 think when they heard people yelling, 'Hey, Virginia!' at me? It just wasn't amusing.

The worst part of it, all my mates, the gang I'd

come up the school with – Barney, Shorty, Lee Nolan, Baz Rainsford – they all claimed to have done it. *Done* it, you know? Gone all the way. Every single one of 'em! Been there, done that. Had her. Poor old Ginny! Still a virgo.

Mind you, I wasn't so naive I necessarily believed them. There's a lot of empty boasting, a lot of vainglory, goes on in school locker rooms. On the other hand – well! You never quite know, do you? They could have been telling the truth. It's not beyond the bounds of possibility. I mean, old Shorty, he'd been going out with this girl from Barley Heath for almost a year. And Lee, he was a real good-looker. I reckon he could get any girl he wanted, that one. And Barney and Baz, they weren't fussy. What I'm saying is, they were just out for a good time. They *could* have done it.

Which only left me. Poor old Ginny, still a virgo.

I wonder if my ancestors ever suffered from being called Ginny? I wonder if my dad did?

That poses another question: which came first, the chicken or the egg? The name, or the nickname? Did I, for instance, have an ancestor that got to be really old, say twenty, twenty-one, and still hadn't done it, and so they started joshing him and calling him Virgo? And the name stuck?

Except they'd have had to be pretty high up the social scale to talk Latin. I don't know as I've got any high-up social ancestors. Dad keeps a shop. Electrical goods. His dad was on the buses. That's a bit of a far cry from spouting Latin.

Still and all, it's an odd surname. To pass on, I mean. Virgins don't usually get to be fathers. Why couldn't I have been called something ordinary and down-to-earth such as Brown or Smith or Higginbotham? I wouldn't have half so much trouble.

I used to study myself in the mirror sometimes, trying to decide whether I looked like a virgin. Did I exude an unmistakable air of virginity? Did I look like a person that hadn't done it?

Except what did you look like when you *had* done it? I couldn't see any of the others looking all that different from me, quite honestly. Sure, Barney and Lee had both started shaving – Barney was so dark he even got a four o'clock shadow about two in the afternoon – but having sex didn't bring that on. Not as far as I knew. Anyway, old Short-ass didn't even have bum fluff, and he claimed he and this girl of his went at it like bunnies every Saturday evening, regular as clockwork.

I still didn't know whether to believe him or not.

If it hadn't been for Priya, I might have joined in and starting doing a bit of boasting on my own account. Anything to stop them taking the mickey. But I couldn't do that to Priya. They all knew I was going out with her; I couldn't salvage my reputation at her expense. It doesn't matter how loyal your mates are, how much they swear to keep secrets, word always gets out. I couldn't tell them lies about Priya, and I wasn't going to pretend I'd done it with someone else 'cos then that would get out, and I didn't want Priya thinking I was just any old Jack-the-lad same as the rest of them. Priya was special. And I wanted to be special for her.

She was in our year at school, but that wasn't how we met. We met at the Copper Kettle Tea Rooms in Parkin's department store. Priya had already been working there a couple of months when I started. We just did Saturdays; they didn't open on a Sunday. The whole store remained closed. They were about nine million light years behind the times and still thought Sunday was a day of rest.

It was a real old-fashioned kind of place. All grannies and great-aunts and middle-aged ladies. They nearly laid eggs when I turned up for work my first day with a stud in my ear. It was like, shock, horror! Like I was wearing a monkey fur jock-strap or a pair of women's tights. I couldn't take it out 'cos it had only just been put in so they made me stick a strip of blue tape over it. Blue, already! This was so's it could be seen if it dropped off in the food. I felt a right bozo.

Everyone else thought it was hilarious. Including Priya...

It's odd I'd never really noticed Priya at school. I mean, I'd seen her round the corridors, obviously, but we weren't in the same classes for anything and she just hadn't *impinged* (I think that's the word) on my consciousness. Until the Copper Kettle. And then she was the first thing that impinged. Almost the only thing. It was like all of a sudden – whizz bang! Zap pow! Wallop! I could hardly take my eyes off her. Dead embarrassing, in one way. I mean, boy, did I ever feel self-conscious! (Especially with blue tape on my ear.) I felt everyone was looking at me, looking at Priya. But in another way—

In another way, it was exhilarating! Like your whole body's on fire. You can feel the blood pounding and hammering through your veins. It's like you've just come alive!

Priya wasn't the only girl at the Copper Kettle. There were three others, plus four of us boys. All the girls had to wear these really dowdy, mumsy dresses, black, with lace collars, little white aprons, starched caps and black shoes. Some it flattered, some it didn't. There was this one girl, Ellie, who was all long and thin. I felt really sorry for her. At least, I would have done if I'd had any thoughts to spare for anyone other than Priya. Poor old Ellie! She looked like a walking beanpole. Her neck stuck out the top like an elongated broomhandle and her legs tottered around like a couple of garden canes with her feet stuck in these great hobnailed boots. Clump clump clump, up and down the place. I couldn't help wondering how she felt, seeing Priya so little and pretty and neat. That gear really suited Priya. Well, I reckon anything would. It had never struck me before, how beautiful she was. Is.

I'll try to describe her, though I'm not too good at description, to tell you the truth. Mr Crawley, our English teacher, says I have no feeling for the poetry of language. He says I have cloth ears. I guess he's right because however hard I try I just can never manage to find the words that I want. It's very frustrating, and especially now. But I'm going to make a real effort, for Priya. She deserves it.

OK, here goes. She has this long, luscious hair, jet black, which sometimes she wears loose, sometimes she wears in a pony tail, sometimes she wears in a plait, and sometimes she does these extraordinarily complicated things with it and piles it on top of her head. She looks very sophisticated when she does that. I like it best when it's loose. Or in a pony tail. But however she wears it, she always looks stunning.

Her face. Her face is…small. Delicate. Tiny little nose, almond-shaped eyes, very deep and dark, like pools of treacle.

Is that poetic? Treacle? I'm trying to say that they don't just look like pools of water, they look like…like velvet! If you can have pools of velvet.

Her body.

I don't think I can write about Priya's body! But if I go back to that first day in the Copper Kettle, the first day when I really and truly noticed her, I think I would simply have said that it was slim and graceful. And *dainty.* That's what Priya is! She's dainty.

Now I'm going to make a confession. I'd always thought, up till then, that I was a tit man. That I went for girls with big boobs. I mean, boobs are what you're supposed to go for right? Cor, look at them knockers! What a handful! etc. and so forth. Eyes on stalks as you gaze at girly pix with your mates in the bog. But then I saw Priya, and tits just didn't seem to come into it.

She's not exactly a D cup.

According to Barney, that's the big one, but so what? What's the obsession with BIG?

I've learnt that what turns me on is small and exquisite. Mounds of flesh are not my scene.

Anyway. That's the best I can do, description-wise. I don't expect old Creepy Crawley would give me more than two out of ten, plus a few sarcastic remarks, but you get the general idea, at least I hope you do. The general idea being that Priya is like a beautiful flower, like a crystal vase, like a twinkling star, and I'm mad about her. So there! Sucks to old Creepy.

The first week or two, in the Copper Kettle, we

didn't talk very much, me and Priya. I was, like, tongue-tied (plus I still had the blue tape) and Priya, she was really conscientious. She took her work dead seriously. Some of the other kids used to muck around, flirting with one another, coming back late from coffee break, skulking in the kitchen instead of getting on with the job. Not Priya. The way she went at it, you'd have thought waiting tables was her vocation in life. (Which I can assure you it is not.) She took real pride in keeping her tables spotless, all laid out with clean cutlery and napkins. They really shone. People always sat at Priya's tables if they could.

One thing that struck me, right back that very first day, was how she had respect for the customers. Some of the others, well, they had their own way of referring to them. The old fart at Table One, or Loopy Lou, or Giggling Gertie.

They took the piss rotten, some of them. But never Priya. Most of the people that used the Copper Kettle were middle-aged or old. Some of them were pretty doddery. They told you doddery old jokes that you were expected to laugh at and long doddery tales about their grandchildren that you were expected to take an interest in, and they doddered with their money and their knives and forks. They upset things and couldn't get the lids off their little jars of Oxford marmalade. If it hadn't been for Priya, I might have taken my lead from the others. I might have rolled my eyes and drummed my fingers and then gone back to the kitchen to take the piss. But Priya was always friendly, always polite, always patient. She laughed at their feeble old jokes like she really did find them amusing. She took what seemed to be a quite genuine interest in their grandchildren. I mean, she can't *honestly* have been interested in hearing how the baby had just got its first tooth or little Julie had won a rosette for her ballet dancing – I really don't think she can – but she made like she was, and they smiled and beamed and were ever so happy, you could tell.

You couldn't even say she did it for the tips, 'cos all the tips were pooled and dished out equally amongst us at the end of the day. She did it because she was just naturally that kind of person.

I started saying 'Hi' and raising a hand as we passed in school corridors. The others started ragging me and saying 'Allo, allo! What's going on 'ere?' But nothing was going on. Not for ages. I couldn't get up the courage to talk to her! It was weird, because I'd never thought of myself as being in any way shy. Sometimes, when the place was quiet, Priya and the other girls in the Copper Kettle would stand in a little huddle talking girl talk. I never quite know what they say to one another when they stand in these huddles, but they always seem to do a lot of giggling, very high-pitched, like the twitterings of birds. It scared the hell out of me! Well, it was more like embarrassment, really, I suppose. I've always had this uncomfortable feeling that when girls get together they discuss boys, by which I mean, they dissect you. Pull you to pieces. Rubbish you. Look at his hair! Look at his nose! Look at the gear he wears! Pathetic.

I guess if I'd been godlike, like Lee, I'd have gone swaggering up and made some kind of smart-ass remark that would have got them all going. Maybe. It wouldn't have got Priya going; I know that now. Lee wouldn't have got anywhere with her! Priya's not impressed by macho males.

But I didn't know that then and it was really beginning to bother me, the fact I was so useless. If it hadn't been for one of the customers, an old lady referred to by the others as Tea-and-Toast, I might never have plucked up the courage to approach Priya. I've got a little old lady to thank for it.

What happened, it was coming up to February the fourteenth – Valentine's Day! Old Tea-and-Toast, she says to me, with a twinkle in her eye, 'And how many Valentines are you sending this year?'

Most of the old ladies liked to kid you about your love life. You had to play along with it, even if you didn't have one. So I shuffled a bit and grinned a foolish sort of grin and then finally admitted that I wasn't sending any. Old T-and-T was really surprised. Or pretended that she was. I'm never quite sure with these old ladies. They've been around a bit. They can really get you going.

'What?' she says. She's got this old quivery voice. 'No Valentines? A good-looking young man like you? Tsk, tsk! What is the world coming to?'

So then I got to thinking...and wondered if I'd dare. Send Priya a Valentine, I mean. I studied myself long and hard in the mirror that night and tried to work out if I really was good-looking, or whether it was just something she'd said. I came to the conclusion that on the whole I wasn't too bad – I mean, I didn't have spots or a receding chin or buck teeth or anything; but was I good enough for Priya? There was only one way to find out. I'd never sent anyone a Valentine before; I only had a hazy idea what you were supposed to put in them. I just felt, with Priya, that it wasn't any use being smooth or smoochy. None of this roses are red, violets are blue stuff. It had to be something a bit more – well! Intellectual. I don't quite know why I thought that. It was just this feeling I had.

I knew it would be a total waste of time asking Mum 'cos a) she's not very intellectual and b) I couldn't imagine that my dad had ever sent her a Valentine in all the years they'd been married. Which is a lot of years. I'm the youngest in our family by quite a bit. I've got three older brothers but only Stoo still lives near, and a fat lot of help he was likely to be. Ditto my mates at school. I could just hear their lewd suggestions. Either that or they'd take the mickey.

'Hey! Guess what? Ginny's trying to lose her virginity!'

They just couldn't understand that there are *other* reasons for going out with a girl.

I spent days racking my brain what to put in that Valentine card. And then I had this moment of pure inspiration. I'd overheard Priya, just a couple of Saturdays back, having a right go at a customer for being sexist. Well, when I say a right go, I don't mean she was yelling at him, or anything. Priya isn't a yelling sort of person. She's very controlled. She was more, like, lecturing him, kind of half serious, half joking, telling him how you couldn't go round patting girls' bums and calling them sweetheart; not these days. Maybe in his day. I mean, she was doing it quite nicely, but she meant it all right. And that old guy, he got the message. He gave this wheezy old chuckle and slapped his wrists and tried to make like it was all a silly girly fuss about nothing, but he wouldn't be caught doing it again. No way!

So, what I decided, I'd do her this *feminist*-type Valentine. I thought it was the sort of thing she would appreciate. I got this bit of card and I drew this girl wearing a T-shirt and jeans, and on the front of the T-shirt I wrote, HANDS OFF in big black lettering. On the other side I wrote this little rhyme I'd made up:

Sexism's *out*
But you are *in*
Please will you be
My Valentine?
Sam *

OK, so it wasn't the greatest, but then English isn't my subject. I just thought that if anything was going to get to her, that might. And I was right: it did! When I went to go home that evening, I found a note in my jacket pocket.

I've never been a Valentine
But I'll be yours if you'll be mine.
Ask me out and I will come
But mark this well: no patting bum.

I couldn't believe it! Priya had agreed to go out with me! All I had to do was ask her!

You'll probably think I'm some kind of wimp, but I spent all Sunday agonising over how to do it. Maybe you won't believe this, but I'd never asked a girl out before. I'm not saying I hadn't been *out* with girls; only I'd never had to ask them. It had always just sort of...happened. Like a crowd of Us

---

* I know you're not supposed to sign Valentines, but I don't see the point of them, otherwise.

had bumped into a crowd of Them, and it had just gone on from there.

I'd never had an actual girlfriend. I might as well be honest. Until I met Priya, I'd never really wanted one. Now I wanted one like crazy, I wanted *Priya* like crazy, and couldn't even think how to ask her!

I wasn't about to consult Lee or Baz or any of the others. They'd only come up with a load of totally asinine suggestions (of the ho ho ho kind), and besides, this was between Priya and me. It was something I had to work out for myself. I really wished I was one of those guys that could just go up to any girl and start a line of chat. Lee could, I'd seen him do it. But he was Greek god-like; I was just me. Not bad-looking, but nothing to swoon over. But in any case, Priya wasn't the sort who'd respond to a line of chat. She needed a more subtle approach.

In the end, I rang her up at home. It seemed preferable to doing it at school, with all the gawkers looking at us and clocking what was going on. I knew where she lived all right 'cos her dad runs the newsagent's in Wythenstall Road. And I was *dead* subtle. I said, 'Is that Priya? This is Sam.' It took a lot of working out, that did.

So Priya giggles and says, 'Yes! I know!' and I say, 'I was wondering if you'd like to come out with me Saturday night?' at which she giggles again and says, 'Why not?'

Girls do a *lot* of giggling. Priya is no exception.

Anyway. That was how it all began. We started going out together and pretty soon we became at item. We did all the things that other people did – we went to parties, we went to clubs, we went to the movies – but somehow it was different. Because Priya was different. She wasn't, isn't, like any other girl I know. She giggles a lot, like I said, just the same as other girls, and she's really feminine, I mean she enjoys wearing smart clothes and looking pretty, but she has a mind. She likes to talk about things. She made *me* talk about things. Sexism; racism. The state of the world. The nature of government. Politics. Euthanasia. Animal rights. You name it, we discussed it. We used to go for these long walks over Barley Edge and just talk, talk, talk.

Mind you, it wasn't all talk. We did other things as well! But not *that.* Never *that.* I dunno why. I mean...I'd have liked to.

But it wasn't an all-consuming passion. It wasn't

something I aimed for, every time we went out. Well, for one thing we were still only fifteen and that's illegal, doing it when you're only fifteen, not that it ever seemed to have stopped Lee or the others. *If* they're to be believed, which at times I seriously doubt. But for another, it's a myth that all guys are raging beasts out to rape and pillage. It really is. Unless I'm peculiar (which I don't think I am).

OK, we fantasise. I've fantasised with the best of them. And yes, OK, there are some girls you only go with for one thing, 'cos apart from that one thing you find them dead boring. Like they probably find you, 'cos they're only going with you for one thing, too. Except mostly it's not the same thing. They want a bloke as some kind of status symbol: you want a girl as some kind of sex object.

But it wasn't like that with Priya and me. It sounds really corny, I know, but I respected her too much. That's why I couldn't join in with the others and pretend we'd done it when we hadn't. I'm not saying it didn't ever cross my mind, because it did. The thought of sex, I mean. I used to lie in bed and dream about it, if you want to know the truth. And we came pretty close once or twice. I mean, like...

pretty close! Priya, she was tempted just as much as me. She might look all meek and mild, but she wanted it! It got so's I started carrying condoms with me, just in case. But I wouldn't ever have pushed her. I swear I wouldn't ever have done that.

And in the end I didn't have to, 'cos in the end it she was the one that pushed me...

Chapter Two

The twenty-first of February: a momentous date! The most significant in my life so far. On that date I ceased to be Virginia...

It was a year almost to the day since I'd plucked up the courage to send Priya a Valentine card. We were just sixteen, and we thought the world was going to end.

I won't bore you with the details. Memories are short, and anyhow it's not important. I mean, like, it's happened before and it'll happen again. Seems it never stops happening. Could have been the Russians, could have been the Chinese, could have been anyone. Just on this occasion it happened to be us (meaning the Brits) and of course the Yanks. If they're going in, the Brits'll go with them. You can just bet! Me and Priya had long discussions about the prospect of war. Priya said if the government ever tried to call people up, she would refuse to fight.

'I'd be a conscientious objector. I'm not going out and killing people.'

I said, 'You mean, you'd rather let them kill you?'

But Priya tossed her head and said it wasn't that simple.

'It's not that cut-and-dried. It's like that stupid question they used to ask people in the First World War. People that wouldn't fight. They used to ask them, what would you do if a German soldier tried to rape your sister?'

'Well?' I said. 'What *would* you do?'

'What would you?' said Priya.

I didn't try saying, 'I haven't got a sister.' Priya doesn't have much patience with that sort of smart mouth stuff. I'd learnt by now that you really have to be on your toes when you're arguing with her. She's cleverer at it than I am. But she's used to in-depth discussions. They do it all the time in her house, her mum and dad and her brother, Yogesh. They're great talkers. We never really talk about anything in our family.

So I told her that my answer to her question would be: 'Brute force! I'd kill the bastard, if necessary.'

'Wouldn't anyone?' said Priya.

'Even you?'

'Of course even me!'

'In that case –' I jabbed a finger on her nose. Triumphant. I'd scored a point! 'How can you possibly say you'd be a conscientious objector?'

'*Because.* I told you.' She grabbed my finger and held on to it. 'Nothing is that simple. If someone comes at me with a knife, I'll defend myself. But I'm not going to go out and kill people just because the government orders me to. I haven't got any quarrel with them! Why should I kill them?'

I didn't really know the answer to that. To be honest, it wasn't something I'd ever given much thought to. I tried talking about it to Mum and Dad next day. I might just as well not have bothered. Mum said, 'He's got to be stopped.' She meant the guy we were out to nobble. 'He's *evil.*'

'Yeah, but that's not the reason we'd go to war with him, is it?' I said. 'Governments don't go to war with people just because they're evil. We didn't go to war with Hitler because he was evil.'

'Just as well we did, though,' said Mum. 'You might not be here today if we hadn't.'

'That's not the point!' I said.

'Isn't it?' said Mum.

'No, it is not!'

'So why do you think we went to war with him?'

'Well, it wasn't to rescue the Jews,' I said. 'That was just in hindsight.'

Mum gazed at me as if I was some sort of weird globule dropped on her from outer space.

'Who tells you these things? I don't know where you get your ideas from. Is it what they teach you at school these days?' And then she added, 'What are we talking about this for, anyway? It's very morbid! Just get on with your dinner.'

'I'm talking about it because we could be on the brink of *war*!' I said. 'And I want to know why!'

'Look, son, just leave it to the people in charge,' said Dad. He sounded weary, as if the whole subject bored him. He'd had a hard week; he didn't need any of this. Sunday was a day of rest. 'I reckon they know what they're doing.'

'So we don't even bother talking about it?'

'They have the facts,' said Dad. 'We don't.'

'So we just sit back and wait till they blow us all up?'

'Oh, it may never happen,' said Mum, cheerfully.

'Eat your food and just forget about it. Worrying never helped anyone.'

I wasn't all that worried, to tell you the truth. I probably should have been, but somehow it just didn't seem real. To Priya it did. Maybe that's because she has more imagination, or more social conscience. I dunno. She's a girl for worrying. Nuclear weapons, nuclear waste. The ecology. Vanishing species. If it hadn't been for Priya, it would all have just washed over me.

Anyway, that was the week before. In my diary, which as a matter of fact I don't bother keeping any more, I've drawn a thick red line and written BLV on one side and ALV on the other. They are my private code. Nobody but me could know what they mean! Before Losing Virginity; After Losing Virginity. My mum could have read my diary and not guessed. I never wrote anything meaningful in there; just boring stuff about school. I junked it pretty soon afterwards.

It was all due to Boris Yeltsin, actually. Me losing my virginity. And just in case Boris is no longer around by the time anyone gets to read this, memories being short, etc., as I said before, I'll remind you that he was the Big Boss of Russia. A pretty important guy, both on the world stage and in my personal life. I have a lot to thank Boris for. If it hadn't been for him, I might still be living in BLV time.

This is what happened. We woke up one morning and there it was, on the news: Boris Yeltsin warns, world on brink of global catastrophe! If Britain and America didn't back off, we could be looking at World War Three. Well, that even shook me a bit, I have to confess. A little local conflict was one thing. But if the big powers were going to start chucking nuclear weapons about –

'It's a disgrace,' said Mum.

She didn't mean the nuclear weapons, she meant Boris Yeltsin opening his mouth.

'Saying a thing like that!'

'He's only trying to warn us,' I said.

'Trying to make trouble, more like,' said Mum.

Nobody at school talked about it because on the whole it's not the sort of thing you talk about at school. You just josh around and talk rubbish is mostly what you do. We're pretty shallow, on the whole.

Which is one of the reasons I love Priya. Priya has *depth.* And she's forced me to have some, too.

I met up with her that day, just briefly, in the sixth form corridor.

'See you tomorrow,' I said.

She screwed up her face and muttered, 'If we're still here.'

Baz was with me. He said, 'Any reason you shouldn't be?'

'No, not really,' I said. 'Apart from the fact they might drop the bomb on us.'

'Who might?'

I shrugged. 'Anyone.'

'Live with it,' said Baz.

He wasn't worried; why should Priya be?

Next day was Saturday and we went for a meal together as usual, after finishing at the Copper Kettle. Priya doesn't eat meat, she's really strict, she won't even eat in a place that serves meat if she can help it, so that meant we couldn't go to MacDonald's, which is where I always used to hang out and where most of the gang still congregated, not that I particularly missed seeing them. I mean, I was with them every day at school. Saturdays were my day for being with Priya. What we normally did, we normally went to this Veggie Bar place in Wythenstall Road, just near where she lives.

That's where we went that evening. They do lots of Indian-type food, masala dosas and biryanis, the sort of stuff we never get to eat at home. (My mum can't handle foreign food. She says it's all very well 'in its place', meaning in its country of origin, but *not over here.* I suppose she's a bit of a food fascist, my mum.) I remember that night so vividly! I remember asking Priya what she'd like to do. Sue Tizzard was having a party; we could go to that. Or there was the new full-length *Star Trek* movie. (Priya's a huge fan of *Star Trek,* believe it or not. She says it's socially responsible and raises important issues. Me, I just like it for the space bits.) If she didn't want to do either of those things there was always the new club that had opened in the High Street. Baz had been there; he reckoned it was pretty good.

Priya wasn't enthusiastic about any of my suggestions. I said, 'So what do you *want* to do?' and she said, 'I want to go home!' I said, 'Home?' feeling like I'd been punched in the guts. Did she mean she was sick of me? She'd had enough of me?

Priya said, 'Both of us!'

'Go back to your place?'

We never went back to Priya's place! Not to

spend the evening. Or mine, come to that. In fact I kept Priya well away from mine. Not that I was ashamed, exactly, but – well. Perhaps I was. I know it's fattist but I can't help squirming at Mum being the size she is, which is to say BIG, and Dad's such a dry old stick. Priya's mum and dad, they're great! They *talk*, they *listen*, they *think*. I'd met them several times, I'd even had tea there. They'd always made me feel welcome. But we never spent the evening!

'What about your folks?' I said.

'They're out,' said Priya.

Her mum and dad had driven up to Birmingham to visit family.

Yogesh was off somewhere with his mates. (He's a year older than Priya. He was at Ridley Hall, the local posh boys' school. Got a scholarship. There isn't a local posh girls' school or Priya would probably have been on a scholarship, as well. Dead brainy, her family. Unlike mine. I sometimes think my lot are brain *dead*.)

I couldn't work out what to make of it, Priya wanting us to go back to her place. It seemed almost like – well! An invitation. Except we'd already agreed, we'd talked about it. *Sex*. It was one of the things we'd discussed.

'It's one of life's major experiences.' That was Priya.

'Absolutely!' (Me.)

'It's not something that should be rushed.'

'Definitely not.'

'I mean...I think one has to be absolutely certain.'

'I agree.'

'As certain as one *can* be.'

'Being certain is very important.'

'I'm sure we'll know when it's the right moment.'

Was she trying to tell me that now was the right moment?

How would I know? Suppose she was trying to tell me and I didn't realise?

Suppose she *wasn't* trying to tell me? And I thought she was?

Just to be on the safe side, I rushed to the gents' lav to check I still had my precious packet of condoms. I had! I'd been carrying them round with me for months. That was all right! I was properly prepared; there wouldn't be any accidents. I was being the responsible male.

But it still bothered me that I might have

misread the signs. As it happened, I couldn't have done. Not even a clod like me. I'll always remember Priya clinging to me, her arms round my neck, saying that we had to do it now, *now*! before the world came to an end.

'I love you, Sam! I love you so much! I don't want to die without knowing what it's all about!'

We really did think the mad bastards were going to blow us all sky high. Well, Priya did, and she'd infected me with her fear. And I didn't want to die without knowing what it was all about, either. 'Cos believe me, I had only the haziest idea. You probably find that hard to believe, but I tell you, my family is seriously weird where sex is concerned. How my mum ever got to have four kids is beyond me. For starters, she's never even seen my dad naked. That's what she told me, one time; almost like it was some kind of virtue. I guess they must have done it under the bedclothes, in the pitch black.

Another thing. We can almost never get to watch a film right the way through in our house 'cos the minute there's a hint of s.e.x. my dad starts clearing his throat and shifting his bum and my mum goes, 'Oh, this is so gross! This is so disgusting! It's not necessary.' And *click*, that's the button on the handset and on we move to another channel. No sex, please! We're decent.

So you see, I was pretty ignorant. Sure, yes, I knew the mechanics. Everyone knows the mechanics. That's the easy part. It's all the stuff that comes before...the build-up. The *foreplay*. How long do you have to spend before you actually go ahead and do it? If I'd got to watch a few more movies, these are things I might have known. But I didn't. I might as well admit it, I was dead nervous. Excited, yes! You'd better believe it. But nervous. Very dead nervous.

One thing I knew, I knew I had to be careful. No rushing at it, hammer and tongs. If this was going to be a major experience, I wanted Priya to enjoy it. I knew girls didn't always; not first time around. I didn't want to put her off or anything.

I tried to be gentle, I really did. But in the end – that is, at the actual moment – there's just no way. What I mean is, you either go ahead and do it, or you don't.

I was sure it must be hurting her, but she said to go on. She kept gasping, 'Do it, do it!' So I did, and what is kind of scary is that while it's happening you don't give a toss about anything else. Not about anything or anyone. For a few incredible seconds, it's like your mind's been wiped out. You're nothing but a writhing mass of primitive instincts.

It's a bit kind of awe inspiring, really. I mean, when you stop and think about it. But brilliant. Dead brilliant!

'Was it all right?' Priya wanted to know, afterwards. 'Was it good?'

I told her, yes. Yes! Yessssss! But I was worried that it hadn't been for her.

She locked her arms round my neck and whispered, 'What do you think?'

'I don't know! Tell me!'

'It was! It was good!'

'*Really* was it?'

'Really!'

'Really really?'

'Really really!'

'And do you still love me?'

'Course I still love you! Do you still love me?'

Did I *still* love her? 'I love you even more!'

'Just 'cos I let you do it!'

'No! Because—'

'Because?'

'You trusted me.'

'I'll always trust you, Sam! Always!'

'You can,' I told her. 'I'll never let you down. I'll never do anything to hurt you...that's a promise!'

I snuggled down next to her, in the single bed in her little bedroom above the shop. On the wall she had posters of The Redwood Tangle, her favourite band, and portraits of the Star Trek crew. She reckons Jean-Luc Picard, of the *Enterprise*, is her ideal man. The guy's old and bald! But he has principles. That's really important to Priya.

She also says he's *sexy*. Way out!

On her bookshelves she had stuff like *Jane Eyre* and *Middlemarch* alongside biographies of people like Nelson Mandela. She also had a Klingon dictionary...

She might be serious-minded, that girl, but she can be really daft at times. I guess it's one of the things that makes me love her. A Klingon dictionary! I ask you!

Anyway. At that particular moment, to be honest, I hadn't noticed what she'd got on her wall or what she'd got on her bookshelves. That came later. All I knew was that we were there, together, cuddled up in her bed. And we'd done it! We'd actually done it! No matter what happened, no matter what they did to the world, blew it up, incinerated it, polluted it out of existence, *we had done it.*

Nobody could take that away from us.

Priya was obviously thinking the same thoughts because she smiled up at me, this mischievous smile that she has, and said, 'So now we know what it's all about!'

'Mm.' I nuzzled my cheek against hers. 'Did it live up to your expectations?'

'Didn't have any! How about you?'

'Well – yes. I guess. Sort of.'

'So did it? Live up to them?'

'Even better,' I assured her. 'A million times!'

We lay for a while without speaking, just savouring the moment; then idly curious. 'cos it was something I'd often wondered, I said, 'Tell me! When girls get in those little huddles and start giggling, is it because they're discussing boys?'

'Could be,' said Priya. 'Could be!'

'What sort of things do they discuss? Do they discuss the size of boys' cocks?'

'I beg your pardon?' said Priya.

'Cocks,' I said.

She flicked a finger at me.

'You mean penises,' she said. And then she

giggled again. 'No, they don't! Why? Did you think they did?'

'I just wondered why they giggled so much.'

'We giggle,' said Priya, 'because boys amuse us.'

'You mean, we're objects of fun?'

'Sometimes. But we quite like them. And what about you when you're in the showers? I bet you discuss the size of girls' breasts!'

'Um...well. Not *all* the time.'

'Just quite a lot of the time! And I bet you call them tits.'

'It's a term of endearment,' I pleaded.

'No, it isn't! It's big macho men's talk.'

'All right,' I said. 'I won't ever call them tits again.'

'Good,' said Priya. 'We've got to have some respect round here!'

She was only teasing me. She knew I had respect for her. She wouldn't have let me do what I'd just done if I hadn't.

'Did it really work for you?' she said. 'Was it like you thought it would be?'

'And some!'

'Was it the sun, the moon and the stars?'

'Absolutely!'

'For me, too,' said Priya. She gave a little contented sigh. 'I could die happy. now.'

'No one's going to die!' I told her. It was something I suddenly felt very certain about. How could they blow the world up when we'd just discovered the joys of sex? They couldn't! No way.

'Next time,' I promised her, 'it'll be even better!'

'Next time?' said Priya.

But there wasn't really any question.

When you've done it once, you have to do it again, just to see if you can improve upon your previous performance. To see if next time you can make the heavens open up for both of you. 'Cos to be honest I had this sneaking suspicion I'd been a bit clumsy. A bit fumbling. A bit too quick. Next time...it would be better!

And next time it is, because next time you can relax a bit more. You know what you're doing, you're not so oafish. This time you *know* you've both enjoyed it, and that makes you want to do it yet again – and again, and again. They haven't blown the world up, in fact the situation seems to have normalised, but you've discovered sex and it's heady and it's intoxicating and you've got high on it.

But it's not easy, when you're just sixteen, to find

a place where you can do it. Priya's mum and dad went up to Birmingham once a month but my mum and dad never went anywhere. Just sat home and gormed at the telly. I could just see their reaction if I tried taking Priya up to my room Filth! Filth! Depravity and filth!

As a matter of fact, I'd never taken Priya home with me at all. I don't know why. I mean, I'd never sat down and analysed why. I think maybe it was to do with the fact that my feeling for Priya was something so precious, I couldn't bear the thought of it being contaminated in any way. The thought of Mum, tight-lipped, saying to Dad, 'You don't think they're up to anything, do you?' Like it was something dirty, something to be ashamed of.

Or was it just the thought of Mum, full stop? You kind of get used to your own mum, but...she is awfully big. Well! When I say big, I guess I mean fat.

My mum is FAT.

I mostly never bring people home. I used to; when I was younger. One time I was at juniors she said I could have a party – the last one I ever had. I didn't want any more after that. I told Mum I was too old for them. All these kids from my class came along and we had a really good time, what I *thought* was a really good time, I mean that was how it seemed while it was happening. Mum was fun and the food was ace and we played loads of games. Mum really tried. She really got into the spirit of the thing. It was way the best party I'd ever been to.

Then come Monday, in the playground, I caught one of the kids pretending to be Sam's mum. He'd taken a couple of footballs and stuffed one up his sweater and one down his pants and was waddling to and fro with his feet splayed out and his arms waving like flippers. He was doing it really well. Everyone was laughing. I guess I'd have laughed, too, if it hadn't been my mum.

After that, I'd stopped bringing people home. So Priya and I never went back to my place. Priya asked me once, she said, 'Wouldn't your mum like it? You going out with me?' I told her not to be so daft. I made an excuse. I said, 'It's dead boring round our place. Dead dull. We wouldn't want to go back there.'

Fortunately we were having really freak weather, back last March. Almost like summer it was, and we found ourselves a place up on the Edge, amongst the bracken. We went there a *lot*!

I don't want to make it sound squalid, like it was just this physical thing we'd got hooked on. It wasn't! There was more to it than that. The physical thing was...yes! All it's cracked up to be, and more. But what was almost best about it was being close to Priya. Making her happy. Lying in each other's arms afterwards, felling this great surge of love and contentment. Nothing else mattered; just being with Priya.

'When we are old,' murmured Priya, 'we shall remember this.'

'We'll be old together,' I urged.

But we couldn't really imagine it...being old! Here and now was what counted.

'Just us, the two of us.'

'And nobody else.'

'Ever!'

All I wanted to do was be with Priya, and protect her. Which is pretty damned ironic, when you think what happened.

But I haven't got to that part yet. I guess I'm trying to put it off. I'm still way back last spring, in our nest in the bracken.

Sometimes to my frustration it rained, and then we couldn't do it. We had to go to the movies instead, and just hold hands.

'I suppose now you'll be all twitchy,' I remember Priya grumbling to me one time.

'Well, won't you?' I said.

'Me? No!' she tossed her head. 'I'm not fixated!'

'But you do like it, though.' I tipped her face towards me. 'Admit it! You wouldn't want to be a nun.'

'Couldn't be anyhow,' retorted Priya. 'Not a Christian!'

It always got me when she said things like that. I kept forgetting she was Indian and came from another culture. Priya's family seemed so normal, compared to mine. You'd have thought it would be the other way round. That is, that my family would be the normal ones – normal for this country, is what I'm trying to say – and Priya's that would be different. But I just felt at home with them from the word go. I know they're Hindus but they're not what you'd call religious. I mean, apart from being vegetarians, which some Hindus are and some Hindus aren't. Whereas my lot – well! They don't go to church or anything, but they're so...*narrow.* Dad especially, but even my brothers. Well, two of them. Even Mum, in spite of having had four kids.

I reckoned Mum would have a fit if she'd known what was going on. That's the way she would have thought of it: something going on.

What was going on was nothing to do with Mum. It was something wonderful and – and *pure.* I truly believe that.

And it was just between Priya and me.

Chapter Three

It was my fault. It was all my fault. I'm not even going to try putting any of it on to Priya. *If only she'd done what I wanted her to do.* If only this, if only that.

I was the one to blame.

The other day, in English, we were reading Oscar Wilde. *The Ballad of Reading Gaol* – or 'Reeding Gole', as Gemma Watkin called it. I wasn't paying too much attention to be honest (English not being my subject) until we came to this bit where he says, 'Each man kills the thing he loves.' That bit really got to me. I copied it out afterwards.

Yet each man kills the thing he loves,
By each let this be heard.
Some do it with a bitter look,
Some with a flattering word.
The coward does it with a kiss,
The brave man with a sword.

I did it with all three. Bitter look. Flattering word. *Kiss.* Priya says that she was just as much to blame as I was, but I can't accept that. I was the one that whined and begged and pleaded. It was a form of bullying. And I very nearly did kill Priya. I ground her down. I almost destroyed her.

How it all started, it started with me nagging at her to go on the pill. Her mum and dad were off on one of their trips to Birmingham, and we were in her bedroom with all its books and posters. All her Trekkie stuff. I used to tease her about being a Trekkie but she stuck up for herself. She said it wasn't any dafter than being a Man. U. supporter when you don't even live in Manchester.

Not that I am a supporter. I mean, not seriously. I've never even seen them except on telly. I haven't got the scarf or anything.

But then, as Priya said, she hadn't got the uniform.

'I'm not a nutter. I just like watching it.'

'Same here,' I said. 'I just like watching them.'

Priya said that was why we got on together: we were both well balanced.

'If I was obsessed by one thing and you were obsessed by another, it wouldn't work.'

'That's right,' I said. 'We both have to be obsessed by the same thing!'

I was only joking; we weren't really obsessed. Only with each other. So why – why, why, *why* – did I have to go and ruin it all? Why, just for starters, when Priya said she didn't want to go on the pill, couldn't I just let it drop? Instead of trying to lay this guilt trip on her?

'It's disgusting using those things! Poxy condoms. They take away half the pleasure.'

'You mean, you're not enjoying it any more?'

I remember her eyes, wide and troubled. It really bothered her, the thought I might not be enjoying it. I said, 'Of course I'm enjoying it, but I could enjoy it even *more.*' And then even I felt a bit gross, a bit insensitive, and quickly added, 'So could you!'

Priya crinkled her forehead. 'I can't imagine enjoying it more.'

Neither could I, if I'm honest. It's just that I'd heard the others going on about it – riding bareback was the expression Lee used – and I'd greedily latched on to the idea. If there was more fun to be had, why not have it?

'It'd be safer, too,' I urged.

'How would it be safer?'

'Condoms can get holes in.'

'You're just saying that to frighten me!'

'I'm saying it because it's true.'

'It's not true! How could they get holes in them? You're just trying to make me do something I don't want to do!'

'But why don't you want to?' I was genuinely flummoxed. To me it seemed so obvious. We were in a stable relationship, we'd been going out for over a year. We loved each other! It was the next logical step.

'I haven't got AIDS,' I said, 'if that's what you're thinking.'

'Of course I don't think you've got AIDS!'

'I hardly could have. You're the only girl I've ever been with.'

'You're the only boy I've ever been with.'

'So do you believe me?'

'You know I believe you!'

'So what is the problem?'

'Me,' said Priya. 'I'm the problem. I just don't want to!'

She was becoming really distressed. But even then I couldn't let it drop.

'All you'd have to do is just go to your doctor and

ask him to put you on it. I'll come with you, if you like.'

'I can't! He's a friend of my family. He might tell them.'

'Of course he wouldn't tell them! Things like that, they're confidential. They're not allowed to tell. Not if you're over age.'

'He could,' said Priya. 'You don't understand! This is a very tight-knit community. Honestly! People gossip like crazy. Everyone knows everyone else's business. You can't keep any secrets, hardly.'

I knew that she was scared of gossip. Going back to her place on a Saturday evening was like being in some kind of spy movie. We always had to slink in through the yard in case someone saw us. But in this case I thought she was fussing unnecessarily. I was pretty sure a doctor wouldn't tell. But even when I suggested going to a different one, she still wouldn't budge. She just didn't want to do it. She said it would be 'too embarrassing'.

That brought me up short, that did. I'd never thought of Priya as being bashful. This was the girl who'd discuss anything and everything. Including stuff that would make my mum and dad curl at the edges. I was totally baffled. So when I tried another approach. One that even at the time I knew was shitty.

'You mean, you won't even do it for me?'

'*Sam!*' Priya looked at me, reproachfully.

'Doesn't seem much to ask,' I said. 'You don't think I enjoy wearing these things, do you?'

'I –' She turned her head on the pillow. I was half sitting up, leaning on one elbow, looming over her. 'I don't see they can make that much difference!'

'Well, they do. Just think about it! You can't feel anything properly.'

Priya bit her lip and said nothing. She hadn't any arguments. She couldn't have: there weren't any. Well, that's what I reckoned at the time. I guess she could have found plenty if she'd really put her mind to it. Priya can always find arguments! She just didn't want to upset me.

'Plus I'm the one that has to go and buy them,' I said. 'How do you think that feels?'

'I thought boys liked doing that sort of thing.'

'What made you think that?'

'I thought it made them feel...macho.'

'Is that what you reckon I want to feel?'

'Well...n-no. Not exactly.'

We'd had this conversation before. Priya doesn't

go for macho men. We'd never have become an item if I'd been macho. She likes men who are *gentle* and *sensitive* and *think*.

I've always tried to live up to her expectations.

'I just thought it was…easier for you,' said Priya.

I said, 'It embarrasses the hell out of me, if you want to know.'

That wasn't even true; you can get the things out of slot machines. I was just trying to manipulate her. Trying to lay this guilt trip on her. The name of the game was gratification. Mine, naturally; not Priya's. Though I did want her to enjoy herself, too! And if using the pill would make it better for me, wouldn't it make it better for her, as well?

That's the way I try to rationalise it.

There are some girls would have told me where to get off. Not Priya. It's pathetically easy to make her feel guilty; I hadn't realised it until then. Strange for someone who can be so fierce in argument. It's this conscience of hers. She just meekly accepted that she was the one causing all the problems.

'You should have told me before,' she said. 'I never thought! I'll get them in future.'

'What's the point of that?' I said. Totally

ungracious. I actually managed to shame myself. 'I don't see why you should have to be embarrassed,' I mumbled.

'Well, but why should you?' retorted Priya. 'Just because you're a boy, that's no reason you should have to do it all the time. We both have to take responsibility, otherwise it's not fair.'

This is what I mean about her conscience. She wouldn't go on the pill, so she had to share the embarrassment of buying condoms.

'It's all right,' I muttered. 'I don't mind doing it. I just thought...if you *were* to go on the pill –'

I paused; hopeful even now.

'I'm sorry,' whispered Priya. 'Please don't make me!'

Make her? She really thought that I would try and *make* her? That shook me. I was obviously coming across as some kind of gung-ho yob from the Stone Age. Some kind of low-life scum that thought women were only there to serve men.

I don't think that; I truly don't. I didn't even before I met Priya. I have always fought very hard against being sexist. It's not easy, coming from the family that I come from. You'll never believe this, but my mum actually rang up a radio station one time and said that a woman's place is in the home. She said that women were made to have children and to look after men. She did! That is exactly what she said. Her very words.

'We don't have the brains to do men's work.'

The guy taking the calls couldn't believe it! He thought it was some kind of a wind-up. But that is my mum for you.

My dad, now, he never says anything. Strong and silent, he is. Leaves all the vocal stuff to Mum. I tell you, we're a right strange lot in my family.

Anyway, I felt really bad about hassling Priya like that. I wanted to do something to make it up to her, like buy her something, maybe, only I couldn't think what to get. If I'd have asked Mum she'd have said flowers or chocolates, 'cos that's what my dad brings home every Saturday for her: a bunch of flowers and a box of chocolates. Every Saturday for thirty years! It's kind of touching really, I suppose, but Priya's not a great chocolate eater and I know for a fact she doesn't like cut flowers. She says once they're cut they're dying. She reckons they ought to be left where they are, to live out their lives in peace.

I wanted to get her something different.

Something that would be special, just for Priya.

What I did, in the end, I bought her a book. It was by this woman writer called Alice Walker that's American and that I've never read but apparently she's pretty well known (to people that read books) and she just happens to be one of Priya's all-time favourite authors. According to Priya, she's really cool. So I went to our local bookshop to see what they'd got. I did it after school when two of the guys were with me. Lee and Bazza. They seemed to think it was seriously peculiar.

'This really calls in to question the whole nature of your relationship,' said Baz.

I said 'What do you mean?'

'Well! A book. I ask you!'

'I upset her,' I said. 'It's just my way of saying sorry.'

They looked at each other. Lee shook his head.

'Once a virgo always a virgo.'

'Virgo by name, virgo by nature.'

I said, 'Listen, you!'

'What? What?' They danced round me in the bookstore. Bookstores are not places for dancing in. I could see an assistant giving us the eye.

'Just shut up,' I said. I gave them a shove, towards

the exit. 'I happen to believe in having relationships that exist on more than one level.'

Hah! That got them. They didn't know what to say to that.

'Is he trying to tell us he's not a virgo?' hissed Baz.

'Or is he trying to tell us it's all in the mind?'

'You mean, like…what's the word?'

'What word?'

'What you said.'

'What did I say?'

'All in the mind!'

'No sex.'

'Right.'

'Right!'

'So what is it?'

'I dunno.'

'Course you know! There's a word.'

'What's it begin with?'

'Uh…p?'

Silence, while they both exercise their mega-size brains.

'Got it!'

'What?'

'Platonic!'

'Oh! Yeah. Right!'

'Morons,' I said.

Priya was dead pleased with her Alice Walker. Books really turn her on.

'Oh, *Sam!*' She flung her arms round my neck. 'Thank you!'

I blushed; I don't know why. It's not something I do much of as a rule.

'Just wanted to show you I'm not an actual bonehead,' I mumbled.

'I never thought you were!'

'I'm sorry I went on at you.'

'You didn't go on at me. Or if you did, I probably deserved it. I know I'm being utterly stupid. It's just – oh, I don't know! Some silly sort of hang-up.'

'That's OK. We're all allowed to have hang-ups,' I said.

'What hang-ups have you got?'

'Me?' I grinned. 'Falling for someone who does nothing but lecture me.'

'I don't lecture you!'

'Oh, no? Every time I open my mouth you tell me I'm being racist or sexist or—'

'I *never* told you you were being racist!'

'Sexist.'

'Yes. Well. *Sexist.* It's very difficult for men not to be. They're so used to ruling the world. This whole society is like one big football game!'

We were back on line. Back to our usual sparring and jousting. Priya had forgiven me for trying to bully her, I'd forgiven her for being pig-headed. Like I said, we're all entitled to our hang-ups. Even Priya couldn't be rational all the time. None the less, it niggled at me. I tried not to let it, but it still did. Every time I tore open one of those little foil packs, I couldn't help the thought flitting through my mind: why *can't* she go on the pill? It always left just a faint trail of irritation behind.

I'm not proud of saying this. But I think one has to be truthful.

I'm not proud of the next bit, either.

I don't really want to write the next bit. It was a Saturday. Back last July. Priya's mum and dad had gone to Birmingham. Yogesh was driving them. He wanted to put in some mileage before he took his test.

Priya very nearly went, as well. Changed her mind at the last minute.

'I hate sitting in the car for hours on end, and besides, I'd rather be with you!'

Saturdays were our only time. They were precious. But because I'd thought she was going with her family, I hadn't brought any condoms. I had a whole unopened pack in my bedroom (stuffed into the toe of one of my football boots. Mum has a tendency to prowl when I'm out). Unfortunately, I didn't remember until it was too late.

What I mean is, by the time I realised they were still in the toe of my football boot and not in my pocket, we'd almost passed the point of no-return.

I guess it was bound to happen, one day.

Priya still reckons it was her fault as much as mine. She says, 'If I'd gone on the pill when you asked me.' And, 'I didn't have to let you do it. I could have stopped you.' But I was the one who assured her it would be all right. I knew about these things. Well, I thought I did. I'd heard the other guys. I'd read books (I do read books; just not the same ones Priya does.)

'There's this thing you can do,' I said.

'What thing?' Priya was eager, but hesitant. She wanted to do it, all right, but not without protection.

'You can, like...pull it out,' I said.

She looked at me, uncertain. 'Are you sure?'

'Sure I'm sure! People do it all the time. It's an accepted method of contraception.'

'You promise?'

'I promise!'

I gave her my word, and I let her down. I meant to do it, I swear I did! But it's not that easy. You get kind of...carried away. It's what I said, about your mind being wiped out. It's one of the aspects of sex that makes it exciting. But it also makes it dangerous. You just can't rely on yourself.

They didn't say this in the books I read. They just said it was one of the things you could do.

You can't go by books. You have to find out for yourself. And sometimes, like with me and Priya, the way you find out is the hard way.

I'll tell you what really gutted me. What really gutted me was Priya, putting her trust in me. Relying on me. She giggled afterwards and said, 'All that fuss you made!' She meant the fuss I'd made about her going on the pill. About me not having to use condoms. 'I just hope it was worth it!'

I'd have liked to tell her that it was, that it was absolute bliss; but I couldn't. I was already starting to worry.

Priya said, 'Well?'

'It was,' I said, 'it was!'

'And you did do what you said you'd do?'

'Yeah!'

I just couldn't bring myself to tell her. But there must have been a note of doubt in my voice 'cos quite sharply Priya said, 'Sam! Did you or didn't you?'

'Yeah! I mean, I – yeah, I did! Couldn't you tell?'

'I thought I could,' said Priya.

'Well, I did! It's just—'

'What?'

'It all happened so fast,' I mumbled. 'I'm not sure I...quite did it in time.'

'Sam!'

'Look, there's no need to panic,' I said. 'It's only the once! Nothing's going to happen.'

Famous last words. Like that sick joke about the *Titanic*: this ship is unsinkab-b-b-ble...

But getting pregnant from just one unguarded moment...that's got to be a chance in a million. Hasn't it? Just about as remote as winning the lottery.

I guess that's what they all say.

Chapter Four

'I just don't think you should worry,' I said. 'I really don't.'

It was the following Saturday. We'd finished at the Copper Kettle and headed for our private place on the Edge. I'd call it a love nest if it didn't sound so corny. It was where we could be alone, undisturbed. Just the two of us, together. Priya had seemed in a real hurry to get there. I could think of only one reason: she wanted me!

I guess that sounds arrogant. But I didn't mean it arrogantly. I wasn't feeling arrogant. I was feeling incredibly fond of her. And this time I'd made sure I'd brought something with me. We weren't having a repeat of last week. No way!

We weren't having a repeat of last week full stop. Priya said she didn't feel like it. She said that wasn't the reason she'd come here.

'Oh. Well. OK,' I said. I was a bit pole-axed, to tell

the truth. I guess I'd been doing a bit of fantasising. I mean...it was going to be ages before we'd have another chance! Priya was flying off to India next day with her family. They were going to be away for almost two whole months. How would I survive?

I guess my face must have fallen. Priya said, 'Sam, I'm sorry! But I just wanted for us to be alone.'

'So we're alone!' I said.

Now what?

'I've been having nightmares,' said Priya.

'Nightmares?' I said. 'Why?'

'You know why!'

'You mean...because of what we did?'

'It's scary!'

'Oh, look, nothing's going to happen,' I said. 'Honest!'

'How do you know?'

That's when I told her I didn't think she should worry.

'I mean, come on! It's a chance in a million. In a million million!'

I wasn't getting at her, I was just trying to reassure her. Trying to cheer her up.

'It wasn't like it was a bad time of the month or anything.'

Priya remained silent.

'Well, it wasn't,' I said, 'was it?'

She hunched a shoulder. 'Could have been.'

'What do you mean, could have been?' Either it had been or it hadn't. She ought to know. 'Was it or wasn't it?' She'd got me nervous now. 'Tell me!'

'I don't know! I don't know what's a bad time and what isn't!'

That flabbergasted me, that did. I thought all girls knew things like that. I thought they learnt it practically in the cradle. Especially a girl like Priya. I mean, there she was, dead brainy – and didn't even know about the workings of her own body!

Sometimes people that are dead brainy just have no common sense at all.

'All I know is,' she said, 'there isn't any *safe* time.'

'Course there is!'

'What do you know about it?'

'A lot more than you! Obviously!'

I just said it, like, joking. I didn't want her to think I was mad at her. But she didn't even smile.

'Why did we do it?' she wailed. 'We must have been mad!'

'Everybody slips up sometimes. It doesn't mean anything's going to happen!'

I slid my arm round her and tried to cuddle her, but she didn't respond.

'Priya! It'll be all right,' I said. 'I promise!'

'Suppose it *isn't*?'

'It will be!'

'But suppose it *isn't*?'

'Then we'll be in it together,' I said. 'But please, please, just stop worrying!'

I guess I was being selfish is what it comes to. I mean, I didn't enjoy the thought of Priya being worried, of course I didn't – specially as it was all my fault. But this was our last day together. I wanted us to be happy! Not spend the whole evening agonising over whether she was going to get pregnant or not.

Actually, as a matter of fact, the whole notion was so way out it was pretty well unthinkable. I mean, I just couldn't get my head round it. And anyway, why worry about something that was almost certainly not going to happen?

'Just think,' I said. 'By the time you get back, it will all be over!'

Priya said, 'What will?'

'The panic!'

'I'm not panicking. I'm just scared.'

'Don't be! Trust me. Watch my lips: *nothing is going to happen.*'

Priya heaved a sigh. Then she smiled a trembly smile and hooked her hair back over her ears.

'If we get through this I'll go on the pill. I will, Sam! I really will!'

Priya flew off to India the next day. I really missed her, and so did all the old folk that came into the Copper Kettle. They said things like, 'She's a good girl, that one,' and 'It's not the same without Priya.'

It wasn't. I went out with the gang, back to all our old haunts, and they joshed me about being a bachelor again, like I was some old married man been let off his string. It was OK, I guess. I mean, I quite enjoyed it. All lads together, it made a change. But I couldn't have gone back to it full time. Not after being with Priya.

And they *still* called me Virginia.

Priya wrote to me from India. I'd told her not to send postcards 'cos I knew my mum would read them and anyway they'd take too long to get here. So she sent an airmail letter and Mum looked at the back of it and said, 'Who's this writing to you from India, then?'

I said, 'Just someone from school.'

'Pree-er.' Mum read it out at tongue's length, as it were. Keeping her distance. Just in case. 'Sounds like a girl's name.'

Dead nosy! I won't ever do that to my kids. If I have any. I'll wait for them to tell me.

'I've never heard you talk of anyone called Priya?'

'No, well, I don't necessarily talk about *all* the people I know.'

'Oh! Hoity-toity. Pardon me for living! I was only trying to take a friendly interest.' Mum reluctantly handed the letter over to me. 'Pretty name. Is she a pretty girl?'

'Yes,' I said.

'That's nice. Gone to visit family, has she?'

'Her grandparents.'

'India. That's a long way to go! Must cost a fortune. What does her dad do?'

'Runs a post office.' I wasn't going to tell her which one.

I really didn't want Mum invading my private space that I shared with Priya. I mean, my mum is all right, but what I had with Priya was special, between the two of us.

Mum got the message. She always does in the end. She said, 'OK, I can tell when I'm just being an interfering old bag. Pretend I didn't ask. I know you like to have your secrets.'

Sometimes she treats me like I'm about ten years old. I guess it's because the other three have grown up and gone away. They're all married; two of them have got kids. Rod's in Australia, Kev's down London. Stoo's just around the corner. We see him quite a bit. He drops in most weekends to say 'Hallo' to Mum. But Ros, his wife, she and Mum don't see eye to eye, so she stays away. When Stoo comes he brings the baby. I know I'm its uncle and I'm supposed to relate to it but I don't get on too well with babies, to tell the truth. At any rate, not this one. It's incredibly boring. But so are its parents, so what chance does it stand?

Stoo is my *least* favourite brother. He used to bash me when I was little. Plus he's a real geek. Rod's OK, but I don't actually know him all that well. He was pretty old when I was born. Kev's the best one. He's into computers, so we have something in common. Also, we share the same sense of humour. We laugh together about Mum and Dad.

Unfortunately, Kev doesn't come home that often. He's got his own life, down in London. I really envy him! I aim to go to uni in London.

Anyway, the trouble is, with them all having flown the nest, as Mum puts it, she concentrates all her maternal energies on me. That's why she sometimes treats me like I'm still a kid, having secrets. There's nothing you can do about it. You just have to humour her.

Priya didn't say anything in her letter about what had been worrying her before she went away. I took that as a good sign; I thought it must mean that the danger had passed. Not that I'd ever really thought there was any. At the end she wrote, 'I still love you! I'll always love you, no matter what.'

I couldn't work out why she said that. *No matter what.* I mean, I was glad she'd said it; but what was the significance of it? It almost made it sound like she was expecting some catastrophic event to occur, like her being forced into an arranged marriage or something. I knew her grandparents were a bit old-fashioned. They were the same age as my mum and dad and according to Priya practically lived in the last century. On the other hand, her mum and dad were bang up-to-date. I couldn't see them letting a thing like that happen.

In the end I decided she was just trying to reassure me. *To part might be to die a little* (old French proverb, told to me by Priya) but our love would survive.

I'd really like to have written her back a proper love letter, only, as I've said before, English is not my subject. I'm not that brilliant with words. All I could think to do was buy her a Star Trek card from our local video store. It had a picture of the old bald guy from the *Enterprise*, the one that's her ideal man.

On the back I wrote, 'Love you. Miss you. Want you. Sam.' And then some kissy kissy bits.

I know it wasn't poetic or anything, but it said what I felt.

One day on the radio they had this phone-in, about teenage pregnancy. Mum loves the phone-ins. She's what I'd call a phone-in junkie. She takes it all dead seriously. Any old subject, Northern Ireland, royal family, national lottery, she's got a view on it. Anyone says anything she disagrees with, she's on that phone quick as a flash setting them straight. I reckon it's what comes of living with Dad for so long. It's her substitute for conversation.

So, anyway, this particular time they're going on about teenagers getting pregnant and how it's getting worse instead of better and why it's happening and what's to be done about it. Mum's there doing the ironing and I'm there touching up the paintwork with white gloss, which is something she's been nagging me to do for ages, which means I'm stuck listening to all the plonkers whether I want to or not.

Several callers ring in to say what a disgrace it is ('a national disgrace') and how it's all the fault of

a) sex education

b) the pill

c) falling moral standards

d) the divorce rate

e) the decline of religion

and

f) I-blame-the-parents.

Mum's nodding and saying 'Exactly!' 'Precisely!' 'Absolutely right!'

Then this woman comes on and says that young people will always want to experiment, it's perfectly natural, there's nothing immoral about it, and what we need is *more* sex education, not less. This really gets Mum going! She snatches up the phone and punches out the number, which you can bet she knows by heart, only she's left it too late, time is up, and there's no one she can vent her spleen on but me.

It's disgusting, she says, teaching young children about sex. She's heard they're even doing it in junior schools these days. It's just putting ideas into innocent heads! If it weren't for *sex education* – she says this like it's some kind of obscenity – it would never even occur to them. Well, sex education and television. They're equally to blame. You can never find a decent family film these days. It's nothing but four-letter words and sex.

I know what's coming next 'cos I've heard it before, so I get in first: 'Not like that in your day.'

'No, it was not!'

'No teenage pregnancies when you were young.'

Mum's not daft. She knows I'm taking the mickey, but she can't resist rising to the bait.

'In my day it was looked upon as something shameful, to get yourself pregnant before you were married. Nice girls didn't go round jumping into bed with their boyfriends at the drop of a hat. We saved ourselves for our husbands. Of course –' BANG with the iron '– half the time they don't bother with husbands these days.'

I point out that times change. 'I bet the only sex education you ever had was looking at pictures of rabbits.'

'And none the worse for it!' snaps Mum.

'Except that then you go and clutter the world up having four kids.'

I don't know what made me say that. Well, yes, I suppose I do. I felt that me and Priya were being got at. *Nice* girls don't go round jumping into bed with their boyfriends a the drop of a hat. I really resented the implication that Priya wasn't a nice girl. She had far more principles than Mum and her narrow-minded morality. Priya really cared about the world and the state it was in. All Mum cared about was a few four-letter words and people having sex. Leastways, that was how it seemed to me.

'Go on about teenage pregnancies,' I muttered, 'then breed like rabbits.'

Mum said, 'If you don't mind, young man, there does happen to be a slight difference...I was a respectably married woman.'

'You didn't have to go and have four kids! That's disgusting, that is. Nobody needs four kids. Half the population's already living on the breadline. We're already destroying the planet. It's just sheer lack of social responsibility!'

Mum was pretty good. I have to say it. She took it on the chin.

'We weren't as aware, in those days. Thirty years ago! People didn't discuss it as they do now. All I knew was, I wanted a daughter. I kept hoping.' She gave this little laugh. Almost, like, apologetic. 'But it wasn't to be.'

It had never occurred to me before, that maybe I'd been a disappointment. I said this to Mum, and she seemed quite shocked. 'Of course you weren't a disappointment! What a thing to say!'

'But you would rather I'd been a girl.'

'No! Once you arrived, you were exactly what I wanted.'

'But a girl would have been nice.'

'Well – yes. But I didn't shed any tears over it. All babies are nice, to my way of thinking.'

'Suppose –' I sat back on my heels, taking care not to let white gloss drip off the paint brush. (I am quite a meticulous painter. I can't stand mess. That is why I do it instead of Mum. Mum tends to be a bit slapdash.) 'Suppose you had a daughter and she got pregnant...what would you do?'

Mum puckered her lips.

'Would you disown her?'

'Disown my own child?' said Mum. 'Never!'

'So what would you do?'

'I wouldn't do anything,' said Mum, 'because it couldn't happen. Not to a daughter of mine.'

'Mum! For heaven's sake! It can happen to anyone.'

'Not to a daughter of mine,' said Mum.

That's typical, that is. Just as I think I'm getting somewhere – establishing a relationship, feeling genuinely fond of her – she has to go and blow it. *Not to a daughter of mine.* Other people's daughters. But not mine. 'Cos mine would have been properly brought up.

She was at it again. Implying things about Priya. But Priya wasn't going to get pregnant! We'd learnt our lesson. I was really looking forward to her coming back. I wanted to make her homecoming something special. I went out and bought her the latest CD of The Redwood Tangle and just for a joke I bought her a Star Trek com. badge. I knew she was flying home on the Friday, ready for school on Monday, so what I thought we'd do, we'd meet up on Saturday evening, after I'd finished at the Copper Kettle (Priya wasn't starting back until the following week) and we'd go for a meal and then maybe take in a movie. My treat! We wouldn't do that terrible thing that so disgusted Mum. I wouldn't even hint at it. I wanted Priya to know that I valued her for her mind every bit as much as her body. I felt it was really important for her to know that. I didn't want her for just the one thing. If I'd just wanted the one thing I could have got it from Gemma Watkin, no problem. But there's more to life than carnal instincts.

She'd promised to ring me as soon as she got home. I waited and waited, but she never rang. I began to get really jittery, imagining her plane coming down in the middle of the Indian Ocean or crash-landing in the Himalayas. (I think perhaps my geography is a bit dodgy.)

At five o'clock I turned on the radio to hear the news. There wasn't any mention of a plane crash. I listened again, every quarter of an hour, right round till Dad got in. Mum couldn't understand what the problem was.

'What are you expecting, World War Three?'

'That's not funny!' I said.

'No, well, I never said it was. But I know these things concern you.'

As if there's something odd about it. Seems to me, it's more odd *not* to be concerned. Mum's like a blind worm, groping through life. Please don't tell me! I don't want to know!

'What's up with him, then?' said Dad.

'Oh, ants in his pants,' said Mum. 'Don't ask! He'll only bite your head off.'

By seven o'clock I could stand it no longer. I told Mum I was going for a run round the block and I rang Priya's number from the telephone in the Fox and Hounds at the end of our road. It was Yogesh who answered. He said, 'Oh, hi, Sam.'

Relief flooded over me.

'Can I speak to Priya?' I said.

'Sure. I'll get her for you.'

I should at least have said hallo. Should at least have asked him how his holiday had been. But I just wanted Priya.

'Sam?'

'Priya! You didn't ring me!'

'I know. I'm sorry.' Her voice sank to a whisper. 'I haven't had a chance. Everybody's here.'

I knew, when she said everybody, she meant her

various aunties and uncles and all their kids.

'Sam, I've got to talk to you!'

'So talk!' I said.

'I can't. Listen, I'll try to get out. I'll ring you back. About half an hour.'

'OK.'

I went back home and spent the next half hour hovering at the top of the stairs, waiting to fly down and pounce the minute the telephone rang. Fortunately it's kept in the hall. With the television blaring (Dad is a bit deaf, though he won't admit it) you could have a reasonably private conversation.

In Priya's place, the phone is in the living room so I could understand why she didn't want to call me from there. You can't tell someone you love them with a dozen or more people listening in.

As soon as the phone started I was down there, clawing up the receiver. Mum looked out into the hall but I waved at her to go away. She pulled a face but disappeared.

'Priya?' I said. 'Where are you?'

'In the Veggie Bar. I said I'd come and pick up some take-aways. I'm sorry I didn't ring earlier. I kept hoping they'd go.'

'That's all right,' I said. 'I was just terrified there'd been an accident.'

'No! But they all came round and wanted to talk and look at slides and hear all the news. I couldn't get away.'

'Don't worry.' Nothing mattered, now that I knew she was safe. 'Do you still love me?'

'What do you think?'

'I don't know! I want to hear you say it.'

'I – still – love – you. Do you still love me?'

'Always!'

'No matter what?'

'No matter what.'

'That's good,' she said, and I could hear a tremor in her voice "cos we're in trouble.'

I said, 'Trouble? What sort of trouble?'

'Sam.' She whispered it at me, down the telephone. 'I'm pregnant!'

Chapter Five

You know that feeling that hits you when the ultimate, ghastly, worst-thing-in-the-world, the nightmare you've been dreading, suddenly comes true? The way your stomach starts to churn and the bottom falls out of it and all the blood in your veins turns to water? That's what happened to me when Priya said she was pregnant. Just for a few seconds it's like all the substance has been drained out of you.

'Sam?' Priya's voice came urgently down the line. 'Are you there?'

I took a grip on myself. 'Yes.'

'Did you hear what I said?'

'Yes. I heard.'

'Sam, we need to talk! We've go to do something!'

'But how—'

'Sam, we've got to!'

I hadn't been trying to argue with her; I just didn't see how she could *know.* Not for certain. I mean...these things have to be checked out. There are proper tests and stuff.

I said, 'Are you absolutely sure?'

'Yes.'

'But how c—'

'Sam, it's no good, I can't talk here!' Priya's voice dropped again to a whisper. 'Everybody knows me.'

Everybody knew her, everybody was related. Raj, who owned the Veggie Bar, was married to one of Priya's aunties. Gita was a cousin. Ashwin was somebody's son. I could see she wouldn't want to discuss our private affairs where there was any chance of being overheard. I suggested we meet but she said she couldn't, not right away.

'They're expecting me back.'

'So later! Come later!'

'Sam, I can't. Please don't be cross!'

'I'm not,' I said. Just a bit irritated. So what, if all the family was there? She wasn't a child! Tell them she was going out. It was her right. It's what I would do.

'It's not that easy,' pleaded Priya. 'You don't understand!'

She was right, of course; I didn't. How could I? Our family's not like hers. We don't have big jolly get-togethers that go on all day and half the night. We don't have big jolly get-togethers full stop. We don't really have anyone visit our house at all. Only Stoo. Priya says I'm lucky, but I don't think she really means it.

Sometimes I think it would be fun to have lots of aunties and uncles and cousins, the way she does. I feel I'm missing out. On the other hand, it does have its drawbacks.

Priya and I agreed to meet up the following evening, outside Parkin's, when I'd finished work.

'Will you eat first? In the canteen? I want to go straight up to the hills, I want to be alone with you.'

I promised her that I would, and rather soberly we said good night.

'I still love you,' I said. 'Do you still love me?'

'Always!'

Surprisingly, I didn't lie awake worrying the whole night through. I don't know why. I guess even now I didn't really take it seriously. I mean I *did* take it seriously; but I didn't quite believe it. Once the first shock waves had worn off, I started to rationalise like crazy. She *couldn't* know for certain. There just wasn't any way! This was the girl who didn't even know when her safe time was, so how could she possibly know that she was pregnant? Scaremongering, that was all it was. Just a false alarm created out of her own panic. I'd read somewhere that shock, or worry, or emotional stress, could upset the balance of the body. Priya had obviously spent the whole of her six weeks in India worrying herself sick.

'Now, listen,' I would say to her. 'Just because nothing's happened this month doesn't mean you're pregnant. Anything could have caused it! The excitement of going away. The change of climate. Anything! If you could just *relax*,' I would say to her. 'Just relax and stop worrying. You'll find it'll all come right. Next month, no problem. You'll be laughing! Except that you won't 'cos then you'll be complaining of stomach cramps.'

That's what I would say to her. And then she would pull a face and say 'I wish!' but she would ruefully agree that I was probably right and that she was panicking for no reason, and I would give her the CD I'd bought her, and the Trekkie com. badge, and she would laugh and protest that she wasn't a nutter, and after that we'd have a bit of a kiss and a cuddle and everything would be hunky dory, as my mum would say.

Well! That was the theory. In practice, it didn't work out that way. In practice, what happened is that I got as far as saying the first few words of my speech – 'Listen, just because nothing's happened this month' – when she kind of took over. She said, 'This month? What about last month?'

I said, 'Last month? But it's only been six weeks!'

'Eight.'

'Well, all right, then! Eight. It still doesn't m—'

'It should have happened the first week I was away.'

'Yes. OK. So—'

'So it should have happened again before we left India!'

'Y-yes. Well. It still d—'

'*Sam.* I'm telling you...I'm pregnant!'

'But how can you know? It could just—'

'I did one of those tests.'

'I said, 'You what?'

'I did one of those tests! Those ones you can buy in the chemist.'

'Oh! Well. Those,' I said blusteringly. 'They're hardly reliable.'

'That's what I thought. So I did two of them, just to make sure. I didn't want you telling me I was getting in a panic over nothing. And don't try saying I must have done it wrong 'cos I didn't! I read the instructions really carefully and I did it just the way they said and I got the same result both times.'

Shall I tell you what I almost said? I almost said that the sort of tests you could buy in India probably weren't the same as the ones you got over here.

Priya must have guessed what was going through my mind. She said, 'We weren't in a rural backwater, you know. Delhi is quite sophisticated.'

'Yeah! I know. That wasn't what I was going to say. I was going to say—'

'What?' said Priya. 'What were you going to say?'

'I was going to say…I'm sorry! I'm sorry, I'm sorry, I'm so sorry!'

'Oh, Sam –'

Priya stumbled forward. I don't know how long we stood there, with our arms round each other. If we could just have stood like that, for ever…but you can't escape from reality. It was still there, waiting for us.

'Sam?' Priya tipped her head up. There were tears trickling out of the corners of her eyes. 'What are we going to do?' she whispered.

I wiped the tears away with the tip of one finger.

'I don't know. But whatever happens...we'll be together! I'll stand by you.'

Big deal. Did I really expect that to make everything all right? *You* get pregnant, *you* have the baby – I'll just stand around.

I didn't mean it like that but what else could I do? I could take the blame, but I couldn't actually shoulder the burden.

'Sam, I can't go ahead and have it!' said Priya.

'No-no. No! Well – no. I see that.'

'I'll kill myself sooner than have it!'

I shuffled, uncomfortably. 'Don't be silly. That's silly talk.'

'I mean it! I swear it!'

'*Priya.* Stop it! Don't say things like that.'

'So what are we going to do?'

'Maybe...could we go to your mum and dad?'

Priya greeting the suggestion with horror.

'No!' She almost howled it at me. 'I can't! They mustn't know!'

'You reckon they'd be mad at you?'

'It's not that. It's – they'd be so disappointed! They've invested so much in me! You've no idea. They've worked so hard. All day, every day...for years and years. They want so badly for me and Yogesh to have all the things they never had. I feel –'

Priya waved a hand. She seemed utterly despairing.

'I feel I've let them down. They've never tried to impose any sort of control. They've never been heavy-handed. They've never said I couldn't go out with you.'

I bristled. 'Why should they?'

'Some parents would! I mean... Indian parents. My Auntie Sheela, she thinks it's terrible the way me and Yogesh have been brought up. She still believes in arranged marriages. If she heard about this, she'd crow! She'd say it just proved that she was right and that my mum and dad were wrong.'

'Well, but she wouldn't need to know,' I said. 'They wouldn't have to tell her.'

'She'd find out. There'd be no way of keeping it from her. You don't know what she's like. Oh, Sam!' Priya clung to me, her fingers gripping my arms. 'We've got to find a way!'

'A way to what? You mean—'

'To get rid of it!'

Abortion. That's what she meant.

'I know it sounds awful, but what else can we do?'

'I – I don't know.'

I'd never really given the subject much thought. *Abortion*...it didn't mean anything. It was about as remote from my life as – as female circumcision. Just something a few religious nutters got hot under the collar about.

Slowly I said, 'So...you'd have to go to your doctor?'

'No! I can't do that! You know I can't do that! And anyway, he doesn't believe in it. He'd say there wasn't any reason for it.'

'I suppose –' I said it carefully – 'in their terms, there isn't.'

'In *their* terms. They're not the ones that are going to have their lives ruined!'

'Would it – I mean –'

I stopped.

'Would it what?' said Priya.

'If we actually had it –' I had this idea that saying 'we' instead of 'you' showed a sort of solidarity – 'would it actually be disaster?'

'It would only ruin my entire life! It's all right for you, you're not the one that would have to go through with it!'

'I know that. I know that! But…we could always get married.'

'Married?'

'Why not?'

'Oh, Sam!'

'People do,' I said.

'Yes, and they usually regret it. We'd end up feeling trapped. Then we'd start blaming each other and blaming the baby and – it's a sweet thought, but honestly, Sam, it wouldn't work.'

'I don't see why not. We love each other!'

'I know we do now, but think of five years' time.'

I was hurt when she said that. 'Why should it be any different?'

'Because. I told you! We'd feel trapped. There are things we both want to do with our lives. Go to university, make something of ourselves.'

'We could still do that.'

'We couldn't! That's just a romantic daydream.

Young couple, dear little baby...Sam, this is *real.* I've got this thing growing inside me and if we don't do something about it really really fast –'

I scrunched my fingers through my hair.

'You mean, like...go to a clinic, or something.'

'It's the only way!'

'But –' I moistened my lips. 'Where'd we get the money?'

When I'd started at the Copper Kettle I'd had some vague notion of saving for a motorbike. Then I'd met Priya and all thoughts of saving money had gone right out of my head. I wished now that I'd taken Dad up on his offer of a holiday job. I would have, except that the mean old skinflint had only wanted to pay me £2 an hour. I told him I'd rather stay home and do Mum's house painting for her for free. I mean, there is such a thing as the dignity of labour.

'I've only got about fifteen quid,' I said.

Priya said she had about the same. 'I spent all mine on presents!'

She meant the presents she'd taken to India with her. She'd bought them for her grandparents, her uncles, her aunties, her cousins; just about everyone who could claim to be related to her. She said it was expected.

We looked at each other, helplessly.

'It wouldn't be enough,' I said, 'would it?'

'I – I don't know!'

'I don't think it would.'

I remembered Mum saying how our next door neighbour had had a private operation and it had cost him over a thousand pounds. I said this to Priya, and she drooped.

'We can't get that kind of money!'

'Yeah, but his was bladder stones,' I said. 'Not like an abortion. I guess an abortion would come a bit cheaper.'

It wasn't the same as a real operation. Not from what I'd heard. They just...well. Sucked the thing out with a vacuum cleaner. From what I'd heard. Priya said, 'So, how much?'

'Well! I dunno. But – I mean – people get them done all the time, don't they? It can't cost a fortune.'

'A hundred pounds?'

'Bit more than that.'

'Two hundred? Three hundred?'

I shuffled, uncomfortably.

'Whatever it is,' cried Priya, 'it'll be more than we can afford!'

I swallowed. 'Maybe they'd...let us pay in instalments.'

'Do you really think so?'

No. I didn't really think so. Who'd trust a couple of sixteen-year-olds?

Priya suddenly went limp in my arms. I realised that she was crying.

'Priya, please don't!' I begged. 'Please, please don't! I'll find a way. I promise you!'

'How?' wept Priya.

'I'll – I'll ring a clinic! Monday. I will!'

'And what if they say it's a thousand pounds?'

'We'll just have to get it from somewhere,' I said.

All the rest of the weekend, it was like my emotions were on some sort of roller-coaster. Basically, of course, I felt guilty as hell. I was the one who'd persuaded Priya into having unprotected sex. I was the one who'd given my word that no harm would come to her. But you can't live non-stop with guilt. After a bit you start to get resentful and try to offload it on to someone else. I found I was thinking things like, 'What's all the fuss about? It's only a baby, for

God's sake! Women have babies all the time.' It wasn't like I'd given her AIDS or she'd developed a brain tumour or something.

As for all this hysterical talk of killing herself, that was just plain ridiculous. Way over the top. People were starving, people were dying, and she was threatening to kill herself all because she was pregnant!

Yes, and if she'd only taken the trouble to learn a bit more about the workings of her own body, the same as other girls, she would have known it was a bad time of the month. If it *had* been a bad time of the month. I mean, how was I supposed to know? It wasn't my business to know!

It's pretty horrible, confessing all this stuff. You just can never tell what kind of a lowlife louse you'll be until you're really pushed.

What it was, it was just a way of, like, having a clear-out. Spewing up all the bile. Getting rid of it. Then once I'd purged my system I could go back to feeling guilty again.

Sunday night I lay in bed and tried to put myself in Priya's place. I tried pretending that I was her and that I was the one having a baby. Well, that didn't work for a start. So then I thought how it would be if we couldn't get rid of it. How people would react when it started to show. People talking about her behind her back. People sniggering.

It wouldn't be quite so bad for me. Ho ho ho and all the rest. Boys will be boys. But breaking the news to Mum and Dad…that made me go pretty hot and cold, I don't mind admitting. That terrified the living daylights out of me. Not to mention being responsible for a *baby*, for heaven's sake!

I knew that Priya was right: it couldn't be allowed to happen. There had to be a solution!

Monday we started back for the autumn term. Going in on the bus I came across Gemma Watkin, sitting on the top deck with her feet up. She was wearing what my mum calls clodhoppers. Big clumpy shoes with stack heels about ten centimetres high. They looked ridiculous, stuck on to the ends of her little skinny legs. Like blocks of cement.

'You want to watch you don't go falling into any rivers,' I said.

She looked at me, haughtily. 'What's your game?'

'Those shoes,' I said. 'Mafia surplus…cement boots. What they put on people they want to get rid of.'

'Oh, ha ha,' said Gemma. 'Very funny, I *don't* think.'

Dead quick on the wit and repartee is Gemma. She's got this reputation for sleeping around. I don't know whether it's true or whether it's just malicious gossip. Whichever, she's OK. I mean, she's quite good-natured on the whole. And not bad looking. She has one of these *bruised* sort of faces which for some reason are exceedingly sexy. Purple stains under the eyes, and pouty lips. I guess you'd say she was attractive. We've been in the same group more or less all the way up the school though I don't really know her all that well. I probably wouldn't normally have gone and sat with her.

It was just desperation made me do it. I mean, I'd been awake half the night with my brains bashing themselves against my skull. I still hadn't come up with any answers.

'Can I ask you something?' I said to Gemma.

'Can I stop you?' she said.

That's her idea of a smart come-back. She's one of those people, she can't ever just *talk*. It drives Priya mad, that sort of thing.

'I just wanted to know,' I said. 'You-don't-have-any-idea-how-to-get-rid-of-a-baby, do you?'

It came blurting out of me. I couldn't believe I'd said it. I just couldn't believe I'd opened my mouth and said it. Gemma, she just cackled.

'Yeah, strangle it at birth,' she said.

I yanked at my tie, which was starting to throttle me.

'Seriously,' I said.

'Seriously,' said Gemma. 'Why ask me? You think I know about these things?'

'No! I mean – not you specially. I'm not suggesting it's something that's ever happened to you.'

'You'd better hadn't.'

'I'm not! I swear I'm not! I just need to ask someone and I – I thought you might know. Being a girl,' I added, lamely.

'Funny,' said Gemma. 'I always thought Priya Patel was a girl. Why not ask her?'

'She's not here,' I said.

'Why? Where's she gone?'

'I mean, she's not *here*. Right this minute.'

'No, and she probably wouldn't have a clue, anyway. Little Goody Two-Shoes.' And then she gives me this look, sort of...quizzical. 'What do you want to know for, in any case? You having one?'

'Yeah, that's just likely!' I gave a laugh which I hoped was convincing. 'That'd make a pretty good story, wouldn't it? That'd make medical history, that would!'

'So what do you want to know for?'

'See, it's this cousin of mine,' I said. I said it really earnestly, thinking of the only cousin I've got, which is the daughter of my dad's brother Charlie. She's called Patricia, pronounced Patreesha, and she's got to be forty if she's a day. She's very religious, she's a Mormon and doesn't drink tea or coffee or touch alcohol. I don't think she touches men, either, though this isn't an actual rule of the Mormons. I don't think it is. I think it's just a rule of my cousin Patreesha.

'She's in trouble,' I said. 'She doesn't know what to do.'

'What's she come to you for?'

'We're very close,' I said.

'Not too close, I hope,' said Gemma, and she cackled again. I could have clobbered her one.

'Look, please!' I said. 'This is really important. I promised her I'd try to find out.'

'What? How to get rid of it?'

'She's desperate,' I said. 'Her dad would kill her.'

'Yeah? Tell her to try a knitting needle.'

'A *what*?'

'Knitting needle. I read about it in a book. A hot bath, a glass of gin and a knitting needle. Works wonders.'

'You're putting me on!' I said.

'No, I'm not. People do it all the time. Mind you, this girl I read about, she fetched up in hospital. Dunno what went wrong. Must have pushed it up too far, or something.'

'That is disgusting!' I said.

'Well, you asked,' said Gemma. And then we reached our stop and she swung her clod-hoppers to the floor with a great thump and said, 'Why can't she just have an abortion?'

'Costs money,' I said.

'Yeah. Well. This is it, in't it?' said Gemma. 'Nothing comes cheap. I'd tell her to try the knitting needle if I was you.'

And off she goes, stomping down the stairs on her ten centremetre stacks with this great stupid smile on her face and me none the wiser than I was before. Serve her right if she falls out of her shoes and breaks her stupid neck!

Cancel that thought. I didn't really mean it. It was hardly Gemma's fault she couldn't solve my problems for me.

One thing I'll say for her, she never let on. About me and Priya, I mean. I'd have known if she had. You bet your sweet life! But she never said a word. She easily could have done, she wasn't daft, she knew it was Priya I was talking about. Everyone knew about me and Priya. But she kept it to herself. She never blabbed.

I'll always be grateful to her for that.

Chapter Six

I'd promised Priya I'd ring up a clinic, and I knew this was one promise I'd got to keep. I saw her mid-morning, but only in passing, in the main corridor. We were both with a crowd of others. I mouthed at her, 'Catch you later,' and she nodded.

When school let out at half three I zipped straight down to the local library, where they have a bank of telephones, all in their own little cabins, nice and private. First I had to get the *Yellow Pages* for London. (I reckoned London would be best. I reckoned everyone went to London, just to be anonymous.) I took them off to a table – an empty table. I didn't want anyone spying on me – and turned to Abortion. Nothing! Not even a cross-reference. The first entry was Accommodation.

That threw me, that did. I almost began to panic. Where was Abortion? Did it mean they weren't allowed to advertise? In which case, how did you find out? And then I calmed down and used my brain. I turned to the front of the book and found it immediately:

ABORTION ADVICE

see: Clinics

Pregnancy Testing Services

I turned to Clinics. *Sexual Health. AIDS. Family Planning.* That's no good! OK. Try Pregnancy Testing. *Pottery, Poultry, Power Tools...Pregnancy.* And there they were, a whole bunch of them.

It was difficult to know which one to pick. I scribbled down a few numbers, took the *Yellow Pages* back to the desk and went out to the lobby to find a telephone.

I guess it sounds ridiculous, but ringing that abortion clinic was one of the hardest things I've ever had to do. One of the hardest things I've had to *nerve* myself to do. Stupid, really, since nobody knew who I was. And once I was actually through, it wasn't anywhere near as bad as I thought. I'd thought they'd want to know all the details, like who are you, how old are you, who is your doctor, do your parents know about it. But they didn't ask any of that. They were quite friendly, as a matter of fact.

First they told me that you didn't need parents' consent; not if you were over sixteen. That was a weight off my mind. Next they told me how much it cost. I kind of gulped a bit at that. Two hundred and eighty-five if you were under fourteen weeks, three hundred if you were over. And me and Priya with precisely thirty pounds between us...

I asked about paying in instalments but they didn't go for that. It was cash up front or nothing. So I gulped again and said OK, I'd think about it.

The woman at the other end advised me not to think too long. 'If you're going to get it done, the sooner the better.'

'Yeah.' I swallowed. 'I realise that.'

I put the phone down and went reeling home thinking, two hundred and eighty-five quid! Where were we going to get that kind of money from?

And why did it cost so much? It was only an abortion! Not a major operation. The way I saw it, you walked in, you had it done, and that was that. Back home the same day. A bit like having a tooth pulled. They just sucked the thing out with a surgical vacuum cleaner from what I'd heard. No big deal. They must be raking it in!

On the way home I called Priya from a public call-box.

'I did it,' I said.

'You rang them?'

'Yeah.'

'What did they say?'

'Well, the good thing is you don't need parents' consent.'

'What's the bad thing?'

'The bad thing–' I took a breath.

'Sam! Tell me!'

'The bad thing is it costs two hundred and eighty-five quid.'

'Oh, God!'

'Priya, we'll get it! We'll get it!'

'But how?' Her voice was just a whisper. I guessed her mum or Yogesh must be there.

'We'll find a way. We'll – borrow it from someone!'

'I don't know anyone!'

Neither did I. We obviously couldn't go to our parents, and who else was there? Priya would be terrified of asking anyone in her family, and I didn't have any family. Not to speak of. Old Uncle

Charlie, Dad's brother, he wouldn't give you the drippings from his nose. There wasn't anyone on Mum's side. That just left my brothers. Fat chance I stood with them! Well, Rod was out of the question, being in Australia. Stoo was out of the question just being Stoo. Kev was the only one who'd be sympathetic and I couldn't ask Kev. He'd just tied himself down with a filthy great mortgage. He didn't have two hundred and eighty-five quid to spare. But somehow or other, *we had to get that money*.

'Priya, I'll find a way! I will! I promise you!'

All week long I feverishly turned over ideas in my mind. Money! How did you get any? *Quickly*. We needed it quickly! Priya was already ten weeks pregnant – eleven by next Saturday. If we left it much longer we'd end up needing three hundred quid, not two hundred and eighty-five. And if we left it too long –

If we left it too long, we wouldn't be able to get it done at all. I didn't know how long too long was 'cos I hadn't thought to ask, but the sooner the better was what the woman at the clinic had said.

I didn't have much of a chance to talk to Priya at school. We were in different sets for everything and hardly ever met but on the odd occasion we passed in the corridors, on the way to our various classes, she would give me this look out of those big dark eyes of hers and I would just curl up. It wasn't reproachful; never that. More like...pleading. Beseeching. Sam, you've got to help me!

It really broke me up, that did. I rang her in the evenings, but she couldn't say much at her end and I couldn't at mine. At my end, Mum always seemed to be hovering. I don't think she was consciously eavesdropping; just couldn't resist the temptation to keep wandering in and out of the kitchen and up and down the stairs, carrying towels or pillow cases or armfuls of toilet rolls.

Or maybe I was just being paranoid. It gets you like that, tension does.

'I haven't forgotten,' I said to Priya. 'I'm working on it.'

'I just don't know what to do!' she said.

I hated to hear her so crushed. It was like all the spirit had been knocked out of her. She'd always been the one in control, the one setting the pace, forcing me to stand up for myself, to argue my corner. We'd teased and we'd kidded and we'd fought our battles – which Priya had usually won.

In lots of ways, I might as well confess it, I'd looked to her for guidance. She'd always seemed ahead of me, in so many things. Now she was looking to me. Begging me to get her out of this mess that I'd got her into.

By the end of the week, I couldn't stand it any longer. I came to a wild decision. There was only one way to get my hands on some money, and that was to help myself. And there was only one place I could think to help myself from, and that was the safe in Dad's shop.

In other words, I was going to steal it.

As I once read somewhere, desperate times call for desperate measures.

But in point of fact, in an odd sort of way, it didn't seem like stealing. It seemed more like – well! Just borrowing. 'cos I was determined I'd pay it back, even if it took for ever. I had these visions of going to Dad one day, in, say, ten years' time, and presenting him with a cheque. *Plus interest.* I'd play fair by him. I wouldn't tell him what it was for, though, I'd just say it was something I felt I owed him. I knew it wouldn't be any use asking the mean old git to make me a loan. Dad never makes loans. It's some weird kind of principle. (Weird kind of principles seem to run in our family. It's like my cousin Patreesha not drinking tea or coffee.) In any case, he'd want to know what I needed it for, and that was something I couldn't tell him.

I reckoned I'd take a round three hundred; just to be on the safe side. It was nothing Dad couldn't afford. We're hardly in the upper income bracket, by which I mean we only live in this dead ordinary semi in a road full of other dead ordinary semis, but Dad's a bit of a thrifty old so-and-so. A real tight wad is what Kev calls him. He hoards money like a squirrel hoards nuts – except that come winter the squirrel digs up his nuts and feeds off them. Dad never lays a finger on his money. He just likes the thought of it being there. Some kind of insecurity, I guess.

Anyway. Friday after school I turned left instead of right outside the gates and set off towards The Parade, which is where Dad has his shop. Virgo Electrical, Suppliers to the Trade. He'd been really put out, had Dad, when I started doing Saturdays in the Copper Kettle. He couldn't understand how come I'd sooner work there than help him in the shop. I tried explaining – 'It's more fun, Dad, being with people my own age.' I also added that they paid better wages, but he said I could hardly expect him to compete with a big store. As for the idea of it being *fun,* he couldn't get his head round that at all. He said that work wasn't about fun. Work was about earning a living and learning to accept responsibility.

Me and Dad don't often see eye to eye. I think life's for enjoying yourself. People like Dad, it seems to me, they just live to be miserable.

In spite of that, him and me not getting on so well, I wasn't exactly looking forward to the task I'd set myself. Stealing from your own dad, it's pretty despicable. It's pretty low. I just knew that it had to be done. You reach a stage where you're so wound up you no longer have any choice.

Not that I was aiming to do the deed right there and then. I didn't plan a stocking mask and stick-up job. First off, I was just going to suss the place out. I wasn't that familiar with Dad's shop, to tell you the truth. I try not to go there too often; I find it kind of depressing. It's this long narrow cell, all hung about with electrical bits and pieces, with Dad in his old cotton coat thing he insists on wearing – same as a doctor's, only sludge brown – hunched on a high stool behind the counter, peering out at you like a big spider. Sometimes a little gnome called Sid comes in to help, but mostly he's just there on his own.

The safe's out back, in the black hole that passes for an office. I've hardly ever been in the office. I needed to get out there to check it was as I remembered – safe on table, burglar alarm behind filing cabinet.

I knew Dad would be surprised to see me. I'd been racking my brains for some kind of reasonable-sounding excuse. The only thing I could come up with was the permission form we'd been given for a trip to London the following week. It had to be signed by a parent. Dad always left that sort of thing to Mum but I could make up some story. My main concern was to get out to the office.

As it happened, I was in luck: Sid was behind the counter. He told me Dad was out back doing the accounts.

'Oh. Right,' I said. 'I'll go through.'

It seemed like an omen. Things were going to work out!

Dad looked at me like he was seeing a phantom.

'Sam?' he said. 'What brings you here?'

'I need you to sign this.'

I pushed the form at him. The safe was just where I remembered it, perched on a table in the corner. It was too much to expect Dad to go and open it right there and then, with me watching eagle-eyed to read the combination, but that was no problem. I knew where he'd hidden the numbers. They were rolled up in a dog tag at the bottom of a vase of dried flowers that Mum keeps on a chest in the bedroom. Mum was dead proud of that hiding-place. She knew that burglars always looked at the *underneaths* of clocks and vases, but not at the *insides.* Leastways, that's what she reckoned. She ought to watch more movies!

'What is this?' said Dad. He peered at the form through his glasses. He wears these half-moon jobs like something out of Dickens.

'It's a permission form,' I said. 'Field trip up to London.'

'Why can't your mother sign it?'

'She could, but I forgot to ask her.' That at least was true. It had been given to us on Monday for return by the end of the week. With all the worry over Priya, it had gone right out of my head. 'I've got to get it back by four thirty,' I said. 'Otherwise I won't be able to go.'

I would, but Dad wasn't to know. He leaves all the school stuff to Mum.

'We're going to the British Museum,' I said. 'I'd really hate to miss it.'

'I don't know.' Dad shook his head. I thought he was going to have a go at me for being irresponsible, but instead he said something kind of pathetic. 'The only time you ever come to see me is when you want something.'

'I –' I stopped. I didn't quite know how to respond to that. I mean, unfortunately he was right. 'I don't very often come this way,' I said. 'It's at the wrong end of town.'

'Yes.' Dad bent his head over the form. He was actually going to *read* it! Like it was a proclamation, or something. With Mum, I just tell her what it's for and she signs. But Dad's a very cautious kind of person.

'It wasn't always like this, you know.'

'S-sorry?' I said. I'd been swivelling my eyes, trying to check that the switch for the burglar alarm was still behind the filing cabinet.

'I said, it wasn't always like this.'

'What wasn't?'

'The wrong end of town. When I started here –' Dad reached out for his pen '– when I started here as a young lad, about the same age you are now, we were at the hub. But time moves on. Us old fossils, we get left behind. Where do I have to sign?'

'Just there,' I said.

'Just there...on the dotted line.'

I watched as very slowly and painstakingly he wrote his name. With Mum it's just a quick illegible scrawl. Not Dad! With Dad it's Timothy J. Virgo, written out in full, the i's dotted, the t's crossed, all in proper joined-up writing, nothing slapdash, no short cuts.

As a rule it irritates the hell out of me – which is why I guess I usually go to Mum. Today for some reason, maybe because of what I was planning to do, it suddenly made me feel kind of sorry for him. I looked at the top of his head, where his hair was thinning, and I felt this great surge of – love, I suppose. For want of a better word. Not the searing sort of love I feel for Priya. More the sort of love you might feel for an old dog that's losing its faculties and needs protecting.

This was my dad! What was I doing? I couldn't

rob my own dad! We'd had our disagreements, sure; but he didn't deserve this. He wasn't such a bad old stick! A bit withered, a bit humourless, but really quite pathetic when you stopped to think about it. He'd been working in that shop over forty years! Ever since he left school – the only job he ever had. He didn't know any better; he thought it was his duty. He hadn't any idea of *doing his own thing*. I thought that was really sad. You couldn't take advantage of a poor old guy like that. It would be like stealing the last chunk of meat from a starving animal.

The trouble was, I still had to have that money. And Dad was the only person who could give it me.

'There.' He folded the form precisely in half and pushed it across the desk towards me. 'Would you care for a cup of something while you're here?'

'Um – no. Thank you. I'm OK. I've got to – get back.' I picked up the form and folded it smaller so it would go in my pocket. 'Dad!'

'Mm?'

'If I begged you...if I went on my knees and *begged* you...would you lend me some money?'

He looked up, frowning. 'You know my

feelings about that sort of thing. Neither a borrower nor a lender be.'

'Dad, please! This is serious. I really need some money.'

'In that case, may I suggest you go out and earn it?'

'I am earning it, but I – I need a lump sum. *Now.*'

He studied me a moment.

'How much would we be talking about?'

I took a breath. 'Three hundred?'

'Three hundred pounds? Have you taken leave of your senses?' Dad removed his glasses and pinched the bridge of his nose, like he couldn't believe what he'd heard. 'What need can you possibly have for a sum like that?'

'It's – kind of personal.'

'Are you in debt?'

'No! I never borrow money from people. You've brought me up,' I said piously, 'to believe that's wrong.'

'So why do you now make such a preposterous demand?'

'Because I can't think what else to do! You're the only person I can turn to. I can't tell you what it's for 'cos I gave my word. But it's someone who's in trouble.'

'And you expect me to foot the bill? For someone else's problem?'

'I'll pay you back! I swear it! Every penny!'

Dad put his glasses back on.

'Forget it, son.'

That's all he said: forget it, son.

I ask you! Is that normal? Is that a normal parental reaction? Wouldn't you expect a little bit more? A little bit more *concern*? A little bit more *curiosity*?

I felt a surge of anger.

'Dad, I'm *begging* you! I wouldn't ask if it wasn't desperate. Someone's life could be at stake here.'

Dad raised an eyebrow but said nothing. He'd already turned back to his books.

'It's this girl I know, Dad. She's—'

'Enough.' Dad held up a warning hand. 'I have had enough.'

'But, D—'

'If you need advice, go to your mother. She's the one for that sort of thing.'

What sort of thing? He didn't even know what I was talking about!

I gave him one more chance.

'Dad, I really do n—'

'I said enough! Now please leave me. I have work to do.'

And that was that. End of conversation. Well, to hell with him! He deserved to have his safe robbed. All my life, *all my life*, it had been the same. Trying to talk to Dad about anything more personal than cable clips or fuse wire sent him into a catatonic trance. And suddenly I resented it. I really did resent it. He was my *dad*, for heaven's sake! He was responsible for my being here. And now I was in real deep trouble and most desperately needed help, what did he do? Shut up like a clam!

What was the matter with this guy?

I gave him one last venomous glare, which he didn't even notice, and slammed my way out of the shop. As far as I was concerned, he'd blown it. He'd get what was coming to him. I'd do it that very same night, while I was still psyched up. I'd get the money and I'd ring Priya and tell her she could stop worrying. Then we'd make an appointment at the clinic and we'd go up to town, the two of us, bunk off school one day. And by the time we came home, it would all be over. Priya would be out of her misery and life could return to normal.

It couldn't be simpler! I knew exactly how I was

going to do it. First get the combination of the safe out of its hidey-hole. Wait till Mum and Dad were asleep, then creep out of the house – maybe yank my bike out of the garden shed, save having to walk for miles – go in the back way, through the little window. Switch off the burglar alarm, open the safe, help myself to what I needed, and scarper.

I ran a final check of the details as I made my way home. Was there anything I'd forgotten? Anything I hadn't thought of?

Yes! Gloves! I'd need gloves. They'd know it was an inside job but without fingerprints there was no way they could pin it on me. Sid would be equally suspect, if not more so. After all, he was an employee, and I was willing to bet Dad only paid him peanuts. He knew where the alarm was, he knew how to switch it off. He probably didn't know the combination of the safe but he could easily have kept watch while Dad was opening it one day.

I guess I felt a bit mean about implicating Sid, but since he wasn't guilty there wasn't any way they could do him for it. At least –

Thoughts of all those wrongful convictions came back to me. The Guildford Four, the Birmingham Six, the Bridgewater Three. To name but a few. But nobody was going to frame Sid! This was only petty crime. It wouldn't be worth it. And anyway, it was all Dad's fault.

I really believed that by now. I guess you can justify anything if you put your mind to it. By the time I arrived home, my conscience was clear. If Dad had only been a proper dad, none of this would have been necessary.

All the same, it gave me a bit of a turn when I picked up the phone and heard Dad's voice at the other end. I'd heard the phone ringing as I came up the path. I'd yelled at Mum, 'It's OK, I'll get it!' I'd thought it was going to be Priya.

'Sam?' said Dad. Was it my imagination or did he really sound accusing? 'What are you doing back already?' Just for a second I couldn't think what he was talking about. Why shouldn't I be back? I usually got back *earlier*.

Then I remembered: the permission form. I'd told him it had to be handed in by four thirty. I was supposed to have gone trailing all the way back to school with it.

'I got lucky,' I said. 'I bumped into one of the teachers.'

'Oh?'

'He took it off me. The form. So I came straight home.'

'I see. Is your mother there?'

'Yeah. I'll get her.' I went to the foot of the stairs and yelled, 'Mum! It's Dad.'

I tried to listen, without making it too obvious, but as far as I could make out the conversation didn't seem to be about me. I'd thought for a minute he might be ringing up to complain that I'd tried to borrow money off him and to tell Mum she'd better look into it. If he had I'd have made something up and said it was this girl I knew needed a nose job, or something. I wouldn't have told them about Priya.

But anyway, it wasn't that.

'What did he want?' I said, as Mum came into the kitchen.

'He just wanted to know about the gravel.'

'What gravel?'

'Gravel for the drive. He wanted to know if it had come.'

I still had this suspicion Dad might have been checking up on me.

'Couldn't he have waited till he got home?'

'No, he wanted to make sure they'd delivered it.

If they hadn't, he'd have rung them.'

'Why couldn't you have rung them?'

'Well. I could have. But he was the one who ordered it.' Mum picked up the kettle and took it over to the sink. 'Anyway,' she said, 'it came.'

'That's all right, then.'

We have these Mickey Mouse conversations all the time in our house. Mickey Mouse stuff is all we ever talk about.

I went upstairs, and into Mum and Dad's bedroom. I took the dried flowers out of the vase and found the dog tag containing the slip of paper with the combination of the safe. I memorised the combination. I put the slip of paper back. I put the flowers back. Then I went downstairs and had a cup of tea and listened while Mum told me all over again about the gravel.

Dad got home at half-past six and I waited for him to bring up the subject of me trying to borrow money off him, but he never mentioned it. I couldn't decide whether he was biding his time, waiting till he and Mum were on their own, or whether he was just going to forget about it.

Let sleeping dogs lie. That's another of Dad's principles.

At ten o'clock he and Mum went to bed, same as always. I stayed downstairs watching telly until about midnight, by which time I reckoned they'd both be dead to the world. Then I took the torch from the kitchen drawer, slipped out the back and down to the shed. I had a bit of a tussle with the shed door, which sticks, but I finally managed to grind it open (over the new gravel) hauled out my bike and wheeled it round the side to the front garden.

I was pretty nervous, I don't mind admitting it. I kept shooting these glances up at the house, wondering what I'd do if a light came on. Actually I was more than just nervous, I was scared almost rigid, to tell you the truth. There was a part of me still couldn't believe what I was planning to do. Nick money from my own dad! That was gross. Whichever way you looked at it. What kind of son would do such a thing? And then I thought, a son that has a dad that never listens to him. Never talks to him. Never *engages* with him. When had my dad ever been a real proper dad to me? Never! Not once. Not once in living memory. So stuff him! He'd got it coming.

I made it on to the road without any problem.

Mum and Dad's room remained in darkness. There was still a fair bit of traffic about but I knew The Parade would be deserted. There's nothing there for anyone at that time of night and no one lives over the shops. There are houses opposite, but that was OK. I'd be tucked away round the back.

It's a long haul from our place to The Parade. All the way up Ponders Hill, which has a gradient of one in three.

I guess it must have been about half twelve when I arrived. I wheeled the bike along the passage, leaned it against the wall and hoisted myself up to the small window at the back. It took me some time to prise it open. Wearing gloves makes you clumsy. But I knew it could be done 'cos I'd heard Dad telling Mum only a few weeks ago that he was either going to have to shell out for a complete new window or have a metal grill put over it. The wood was rotten and the putty had dried up, leaving great cracks, so it was no real problem getting a knife in there and gouging out the pane of glass. Just the one pane it was, and the worst part was not getting it out so much as not letting it fall to the ground and smash. Not that there was anyone around to have heard it, but as I think I said before, I don't like mess. I guess I'm a bit of a craftsman, in my way.

Fortunately, I'm also quite athletic. It's not everyone could have squeezed through that narrow space. I inched my way in, head first, and managed to slither to the floor without making too much racket. I knocked over a can of bog cleaner and a bucket but the sound was smothered by the burglar alarm doing its bit. I knew I had to get there and switch it off.

I raced through to the office and dived for the filing cabinet. But the alarm stopped before I could reach it. The light went on, and Dad's voice said, 'Strange time of night to come visiting, isn't it?'

Chapter Seven

'Second time in one day,' said Dad. 'I am honoured!'

There was a silence. I just couldn't think of a thing to say.

'To what do I owe the pleasure on this occasion?'

I swallowed. 'I –'

I what?

'I –'

Dad waited, politely.

'I thought I might have left my maths book here!'

'Your maths book,' said Dad.

'Yeah. My maths book. You know! For homework.'

'Ah! Yes. How very conscientious. Could it not have waited until morning?'

'No! I – I had to have it. I – I had to – to do –' I floundered to a standstill.

'Your homework?'

'Yeah! My homework!'

'In the middle of the night.'

'Yeah – well. Not exactly. I mean –'

'You must think me completely stupid,' said Dad.

I wasn't thinking anything right at that moment. I was too damn scared, to tell you the truth.

'I wasn't born yesterday, you know. I may seem old and past it to you, but I've still got all my marbles.'

I gave a sickly smile. I knew it was sickly. I could feel my lips all palsied and quivering.

Dad shook his head. 'You picked a bad time, son.'

He meant there was a *good* time?

'I'm in the habit of waking round about midnight. You'll discover when you reach my age…calls of nature, and so forth.'

I cringed. Did we have to? I didn't want to know about Dad and his calls of nature.

'Did my eyes deceive me, I wondered, as I idly glanced out of the bathroom window, or was that really my son furtively making his way down the garden?' Dad paused, for effect. 'I looked more closely. It was! It was my son! My son Sam – who ought to have been in his bed and asleep. Well! I put it to you. What was I to think?'

'I thought,' said Dad, 'that this was extremely curious. What could he be up to, creeping down the path? I went on to the landing, to get a better view. I was astonished! He was opening the shed – he was taking out his bicycle. At this time of night!'

Hang it out, Dad. Make a meal of it.

'I watched as he wheeled it round the front. I went back into my bedroom and looked out the window. Just in time to see him disappear up the road! Where could he possibly be going at such an hour?'

I got the distinct impression that Dad was enjoying himself. I'd never have thought it of him. I honestly wouldn't.

'Well! This is the question I asked myself. And how do you suppose I answered? I'll tell you how I answered. I put two and two together, and lo and behold! They came to four. So I woke your mother, I put on my clothes, I got in the car and I drove out here along the bypass.'

Cunning. Dead cunning. He knew I'd take the other route, up Ponders Hill.

'And now I suggest we go home to your mother.

I'm sure she'll be wanting a word with you.'

'Dad, I can explain,' I said. 'There's no need to bother Mum! I told you, it's this girl I know, she needs a—'

A nose job was what I was going to say. But Dad cut me short.

'Please!' He held up a hand. Scrawny old withered hand. But he still had all his marbles even if he did have to get up to piss in the night. 'Spare me the details! We've already been through this once. I have no desire to go through it again. You can speak to your mother.'

He wouldn't let me get my bike; he said I could leave it where it was and come back for it some other time.

'If it's still there,' I said.

Dad agreed that there were a lot of dishonest people about.

'However, that is a chance you will have to take.'

'It seems a bit of a waste,' I muttered.

Dad said I should have thought of that before.

'My aim now is to get back home and go to bed. My sleep has been curtailed and I shall suffer for it in the morning.'

'Well, you get back and I'll follow,' I said; but he

wouldn't hear of it. We were going back together, and that was that. I don't know what he thought I was likely to get up to. Abscond, maybe; or sneak back into the shop and do the deed I'd originally come to do. Not that he'd ever actually accused me of planning to rob the safe. Not that I'd ever admitted it. But he knew, all right; and he knew that I knew that he knew.

Mum was waiting up for us. She was wearing her nightie and a pink dressing gown. It gave me a bit of a shock. I hadn't seen Mum in her night gear since I can't remember when.

I'd forgotten just how...BIG she was. When you live with someone you tend to stop noticing how they look. If anyone had've asked me, I'd have said that my mum was a pretty large woman. But in that nightie and that dressing gown she wasn't just large, she was enormous.

Normally I think she'd have been self-conscious. That's why she never walked round in her night gear; not as a rule. It had to be something fairly momentous (such as Sam trying to rob his dad's safe).

'Sit down, Sam,' she said. 'I'll get the kettle on.'

'Mum, it's all right,' I said, 'I don't—'

'We have to talk. A cup of something helps. Gives you something to concentrate on.'

I sank down on to a kitchen stool and waited while Mum busied herself with the kettle and teabags. Dad had gone straight back upstairs without a word. He didn't want to know. Even now. After all that had happened. He just didn't want to know!

'There, now.' Mum pushed a mug of tea at me. She'd got the biscuit tin out as well, but I didn't feel like eating. 'It's that girl,' she said, 'isn't it? That one that wrote to you. That Pree-er.'

I didn't say anything.

'What is it, Sam? What's happened?'

'I –' I snatched up my mug. Mum was quite right: it did help. 'She needs a nose job,' I said.

'What do you mean, she needs a nose job?'

'It's her nose. She's really self-conscious about her nose.'

'Why? What's wrong with it?'

'It – well. Nothing, really. But she reckons there is. It's sort of...prominent.'

I felt a real louse, saying that. Priya's nose is tiny. A really delicate little nose.

'See, she always feels she's being laughed at,' I said. 'Just on account of it being so prominent.'

'I thought you told me she was pretty.'

'She is! But she's got this idea in her head that she's, like, deformed. She's threatening to kill herself if something isn't done about it.'

'How far gone is she?' said Mum.

'Well, she's – like – suicidal. It's really bad news for a girl, if you've got some kind of facial defect. It can blight your whole life.'

'I meant,' said Mum, 'how many weeks pregnant is she?'

That's the point at which I collapsed. I know when I'm beaten. My mum may be fat but she's not a fool. She hadn't swallowed any of that nose stuff any more than Gemma had swallowed my Patricia story.

'How many weeks, Sam?'

It was like she'd known all along. I guessed Dad must have talked to her and, being pretty shrewd, she'd put two and two together. The news hadn't come as the shock I'd thought it would. She was prepared for it.

'Sam!' She said it sharply. 'How many weeks?'

'I – um. Ten.'

'Ten weeks.' I could see Mum casting her mind back. 'July. Just before you broke up. Before she went off to India.'

I nodded, miserably. Now for the lecture. Disgusting, disgraceful. Filthy. Immoral.

'How long have you known each other?' said Mum.

'About...eighteen months.'

'How long have you been –' Mum waved a hand. A little pink hand, all dimpled like a baby's.

I frowned. I didn't want to think about babies.

'Or was it a one-off? At a party? You got drunk, or—'

'No! It wasn't like that. We love each other. I'd marry her if she would!'

'At sixteen?' Mum's eyebrows shot up. 'I take it you're both the same age? She's not—'

'She's not under age,' I said. 'We waited! We're not irresponsible. This was just a – a mistake.'

'Do her parents know?'

'She doesn't want them to!'

'She may not want them to, but sooner or later they'll have to. She can hardly keep it from them.'

'She could,' I mumbled, 'if we had an abortion.'

Mum froze. You could almost see all those jellylike mounds firming up.

'I'd hoped you weren't going to say that. A son of mine—'

'Mum, it's the only solution!'

'Now, you listen here, Sam. It is never the only solution. It's no solution at all! It's cold-blooded murder. I'm ashamed of you for even thinking about it.'

That shook me, that did. I'd no idea Mum felt so strongly about it. As you can probably imagine, abortion is not a subject that very often crops up in our house. In fact, as far as I could recall it wasn't a subject that had ever cropped up.

This is one of the problems of belonging to a family that doesn't talk.

'Mum, you don't understand,' I said. 'Priya's terrified! She'll kill herself rather than go ahead and have the baby.'

'I don't think so,' said Mum.

'But it'll ruin her life! And it's not fair, because it wasn't her fault.'

'So whose fault was it?'

'Mine, if anyone's.'

'If anyone's?' Mum raised an eyebrow. 'It has to be someone's, Sam.'

'So, all right! It was mine!'

'It wasn't the baby's, that's for sure.'

'I said! It was mine!'

'But the baby has to pay the price? You think that's fair?'

'I – well!'

Mum waited.

'Mum, it was an accident,' I muttered. 'It was just one of those things. We got carried away.'

'Both of you.'

'Well – yes! But me more than Priya. She wasn't the one to blame.'

'It seems to me,' said Mum, 'that you were both to blame. She has a tongue in her head, hasn't she? She could have said no. She chose not to. You both have to shoulder the responsibility.'

'But Priya's the one that has to suffer. I can't let that happen, Mum! That's why I went to Dad. I begged him to lend me the money! I'd have paid him back, I swear I would! He wouldn't even talk to me. He's my *dad.* And I can't even talk to him!'

'Your dad finds talking difficult. He had a very repressive upbringing. I discovered, early on... there are some things you have to take on trust. Like the fact that he loves you. He does love you, Sam! He just can't express it.'

'Fat lot of comfort that is,' I mumbled.

'Well.' Mum shrugged. 'It's the way he is. He can't help it. I've learnt to live with it and so must you. But what you tried to do tonight, that was wicked. Doubly wicked. I just thank God you didn't succeed. Now, I'd like to make a suggestion.'

Mum stood up and brushed the biscuit crumbs from her dressing gown. She'd eaten half a tinful while we'd been sitting there. I guess it's her way of coping.

'I'd like you to bring Priya to meet me.'

'*Meet* you?'

'Why not? What's so startling about it?'

'I – don't know. I –' I buried my nose in my mug of tea. Priya meeting Mum? They had nothing in common!

'When will you next be seeing her?'

'Tomorrow. At work.'

'Then why not bring her back here afterwards, for a meal?'

'She's a vegetarian,' I said.

'So? I suppose I know how to cook vegetables, don't I?'

'But what about Dad?'

'We can eat before your dad gets here.' Dad's

never back before seven, seven thirty on a Saturday. Priya and I finished at six. 'We'll have our meal and leave his in the oven. Then we can go in the other room and talk while he's out here. Your dad won't interfere. Don't worry about that. You just bring that girl round here like I tell you.'

'You won't...have a go at her?' I said.

'I won't have a go at her! Not my place, is it? I'm not her mum. I just want to see her.'

'Well – I dunno.' I wasn't happy about bringing Mum and Priya together. I'd been so careful to keep them apart.

'Sam, you need help,' said Mum. 'The pair of you. This isn't something you can deal with by yourselves. Now you do as I tell you and between us we'll get things sorted.'

I heaved a sigh. 'OK.'

I was still doubtful, but at the same time it was a relief. Just to hand the whole thing over to someone else. Mum would work something out!

'I'll ask her,' I said. 'I'll see how she feels. But if she doesn't want to come, I can't make her.'

'She'll come,' said Mum.

It wasn't till afterwards I realised. Not once, in all our talking, had Mum said anything censorious about me and Priya sleeping together. She'd rebuked me for what I'd tried to do to Dad, she'd nearly hit the roof when I mentioned the word abortion, but she hadn't said a thing about me making Priya pregnant.

There are times when your parents really can surprise you.

Chapter Eight

I was late for work the next day, really late. First time ever.

'I thought you weren't coming!' said Priya.

She seemed quite agitated. Like she'd thought I might have gone and done something stupid. Topped myself, or something; the way she was always threatening: *I'll kill myself sooner than have this baby!*

Or maybe she thought I'd just done a bunk, trying to wriggle out of my responsibilities. Jacked in the job, gone somewhere else. Anything to avoid having to see her. Didn't she trust me at all?

'Catch you in the lunch break.' I mouthed it at her as she sped off to take an order. 'Got something to tell you.'

Her eyes lit up. 'You've found a way?'

'N-no. Not exactly.' I didn't want to give her false hope. 'But we've got to talk!'

'All right.' She nodded. The light had already gone out of her eyes. 'See you later.'

I was really nervous at the thought of breaking the news to Priya. I reckoned for starters she'd be pretty mad at me for giving away her secret. I certainly thought I'd have a hard time convincing her to come back with me and talk to Mum. But she wasn't mad. When I explained how it had all happened – me trying to break into Dad's safe and him catching me at it – she held my hand very hard under the table and said, 'Sam, this is so terrible! It's all my fault!'

'Course it's not your fault! How's it your fault?'

'Going on at you all the time…I'm just being useless!'

'No, you're not. You're the one that's having to cope. It ought to be up to me. I'm the one who got you into it.'

'Sam, you can't keep saying that! We're supposed to be equal!'

'Yeah. Well. Anyway. The thing is, my mum wants you to come back with me tonight. She wants to talk to you.'

'Your mum?' Priya looked at me, doubtfully.

'She says we need help. She says it's not

something we can handle by ourselves.'

I honestly never thought that Priya would agree. I thought she'd say it was none of Mum's business and I oughtn't to have told her. Instead, very gravely, she said, 'She's right, isn't she?'

'Well…I guess.'

'I'll come and talk to her, Sam. But you've got to be there!'

'You bet I'll be there! She won't bite, though. I promise you. She's OK, my mum.'

'And she won't lecture me? I don't think I could bear to be lectured!'

'She won't lecture. She knows how it happened. I told her, it wasn't just some stupid one-off at a party.'

'What about your dad?'

'Don't worry about him. He won't be there. He doesn't want anything to do with it,' I said.

It wasn't till later, when we were on our way back to my place, that I found the courage to warn Priya about Mum's attitude to abortion.

'She's a bit anti. She won't have a go at you for getting pregnant, but she might have a go at you for wanting an abortion.'

'What?' Priya stopped, and looked at me. 'You mean she doesn't believe in it?'

‘Well – no. I mean…’ I waved a hand. ‘She’s got this thing about it.’

‘So why am I going to see her?’

I didn’t really know the answer to that. I guess I was clinging desperately to the belief that maybe, just maybe, Priya would be able to talk Mum round.

‘People can change their minds,’ I mumbled.

There was a pause. I thought for a moment Priya was going to say that she’d changed hers: she wasn’t coming back with me after all. But then, very slowly, she took a breath.

‘OK.’ She tilted her chin. ‘I can handle that. I’ve thought it all out, I know where I stand. So long as you’ll support me.

‘I’ll always support you,’ I said.

It was sort of touching: Mum had gone to a lot of trouble, trying to make herself look nice for meeting Priya. She’d done her hair and put on some make-up, which was something she doesn’t usually bother with. I reckon she must have been really pretty, once, before she got fat. She still has this incredibly smooth skin. I mean, for a woman of her age. There wasn’t much she could do to make herself look anything less than enormous, but she’d tried her best. She was wearing these black trousers, stretchy ones, and a sweater I hadn't seen before, black velvet with red roses. Priya would have looked great in it! But then Priya would look great in anything. Poor old Mum, she just looked – well! Like a fat woman. But a *smart* fat woman. I felt incredibly fond of her.

And she'd come up trumps with the meal, and all. She's not a bad cook, when she wants to be. She'd done this lentil thing, a sort of pie, with mashed spuds on the top. It was really good.

I said, 'Is this what Dad's eating?' thinking that Dad would do his bits if he didn't get his meat. Mum gave me this roguish grin and put a finger to her lips and said, 'Sh! Don't let on.'

'He'll notice,' I said. 'He'll know it's not meat.'

'He'll eat what he's given,' said Mum. 'Is your dad like that, Priya?'

Priya was sitting there dead quiet. As a rule she has these exceptionally nice manners, very proper and polite, but with my mum she was acting like she was really shy. I guess it was because she didn't quite know what to expect. She was still scared Mum was going to have a go at her.

'Priya's dad's a vegetarian,' I said. 'All her family is.'

'Well! That must save a bit of money,' said Mum.

'Mum, it's a matter of *principle,*' I said.

'I know that, thank you very much! Mr Clever Clogs. I was just saying; that's all.'

For pudding she'd done apple tart. She was careful to assure Priya, 'There's no animal fat in the pastry. It's quite safe for you to eat.'

She didn't say it snidely. She said it like she was really anxious Priya should enjoy the meal. It occurred to me that Mum would have loved it if we'd had jolly family gathering like the Patels. She could have cooked to her heart's content. Mum's missed out on quite a lot, one way or another, by marrying Dad. But I guess she loves him.

All through the meal Mum was doing her best to get Priya to talk. She kept asking her these things that grown-ups always ask.

'What subjects are you doing for A level, then, Priya?'

Priya said English, history and economics. Mum was duly impressed.

'Economics? Well! You'd need a bit of brain for that, I'd say. What do you hope to do when you leave school?'

Priya said go to university and then maybe work

for one of the international aid organisations.

'Do some good in the world.' Mum nodded. 'That makes a nice change from just wanting to earn money.'

I could see that Priya was going up in Mum's estimation. I couldn't help thinking that I'd seriously misjudged my mum. For someone who couldn't watch sex scenes on TV she was handling this whole situation with remarkable cool. If you'd ever have asked me, I'd have said she'd go berserk, but not a bit of it. In a strange sort of way, just as I'd had the feeling last night that Dad was enjoying himself, playing me along, I had the feeling that Mum was enjoying herself now. Not gloating, like Dad had been. She wasn't on a power kick. I think she just liked the thought of being...valued. Able to help.

As soon as we'd finished the meal she gathered up the dishes and started dumping them in the sink. Priya wanted to help with the washing up, but Mum said she'd see to all that later.

'I think the time has come to talk.'

I knew this was the moment Priya had been dreading. I wasn't looking forward to it too much myself, to be honest with you.

We all trooped into the sitting room, where Priya and I sat next to each other on the sofa and Mum sat opposite, in an armchair.

'Now,' said Mum, 'I'm not going to tell you that you've both been very foolish and irresponsible because you seem to me like a sensible girl and I'm sure you already know it.'

Priya dipped her head. I reached out for her hand and held it.

'The question is,' said Mum, 'what are we going to do about it?'

Priya didn't say anything. Neither did I. We were waiting for Mum to tell us.

'I understand from Sam that you haven't yet broken the news to your mum and dad?'

'I can't,' whispered Priya.

'Well, you know, my lovey, you're going to have to. They're going to have to know sooner or later. And the sooner the better, I'd say.'

'I can't, Mrs Virgo! I really can't!'

'Maybe you'd like me to do it for you?'

'No!' Priya shook her head, violently. 'I mean...thank you, but please no!'

'They'll take it far better than you think. You'd be surprised! Your mum, she'll be shocked at first, of course she will, it's only natural. But having a baby's only natural, too! When she gets used to the idea she'll probably be quite excited.'

Priya stared at Mum as if she were mad.

'Mrs Virgo,' she said, 'I can't have this baby! I just can't!'

Mum's lips tightened. 'You are having it, my lovey, whether you like it or not. It's there, inside you. There's nothing you can do about it.'

'There's got to be! There's go to be!' Priya's voice broke. 'You don't understand!'

'Oh, I think I do,' said Mum. 'Young people, can't control themselves, take risks – and then don't want to face the consequences. Think they can just...get rid of them. Just like that!' Mum snapped her fingers. 'One minute there's a baby, next minute a corpse.'

'It is not a baby,' said Priya. She said it in these very careful, unemotional tones. 'It's a foetus. It has no independent life. Outside of me, it doesn't exist.'

'So that gives you the right to kill it?'

'You talk about killing,' said Priya. 'Where does killing actually begin? Does it begin with birth control? What about sperm? They're a form of life, aren't they? We don't think twice about killing them.'

Mum made an exasperated tutting noise.

'What about animals?' said Priya. 'We kill them all the time. We *eat* them. Nobody bats an eyelid.'

'That is quite different, and you know it,' said Mum.

'I don't know it! I think it's wicked to kill creatures that are alive and can feel pain. But sperm can't! Foetuses can't.'

'Are you quite sure of that?' said Mum.

'Yes! I am.'

'Well, I shouldn't be, if I were you.'

'As far as we are aware,' said Priya, 'they do not feel pain. But animals do! How is it you don't mind killing them?'

Mum made an impatient gesture. 'This is getting us nowhere! I didn't ask Sam to bring you here so we could get into an argument. I asked him to bring you so we could sort things out.'

'But you're not being logical!' cried Priya.

'Maybe I'm not. And maybe you're a very clever young woman. But there's more to this than just being clever. Priya, my dear –' Mum leaned forward. 'Believe me,' she said, 'if you murder this baby it is something that will haunt you for the rest of your days.'

I could almost hear Priya clenching her teeth.

'Abortion is not murder. And a foetus is not a baby.'

'But you said to me just now –' Mum can be pretty quick off the mark at times '– you said, and I quote your exact words, *I cannot have this baby*.'

'I meant that I couldn't have the baby that this foetus would become!'

'If it isn't murdered first.' Mum shook her head. 'You're just playing with words, my dear. Whichever way you look at it, you'd be taking a life.'

'I would be stopping something *developing* into a life.'

'That,' said Mum, 'is splitting hairs.'

'I don't think so!'

'You may not – I do.'

'Mrs Virgo –' Priya said it earnestly '– I don't believe in abortion as a form of contraception, but I do believe that this body is my body and that it's my right to choose what I do with it. And I choose not to let this collection of cells go on growing!'

Mum gave a little snort. 'That's the easy way out. Collection of cells...foetus. It doesn't mean anything. Try thinking of the end product! Think of a baby – a real, live, breathing baby. *That* is what you're trying to kill. And in my book, that is murder.'

'Mum!' I couldn't just sit by and let her say these things. It was sheer bullying. Priya was already quite distressed enough without Mum accusing her of wanting to murder babies. 'You're not being fair! You're...you're personalising a *thing*. You're—'

'You keep out of this, Sam Virgo.' Mum turned on me, sharply. 'This is between Priya and me.'

Priya gave me a watery smile. 'Woman's talk, Sam.'

Woman's talk? I stared at her, revolted. Since when had Priya subscribed to that sort of thing?

'Joke,' she said.

Huh! Some joke. I sat back, feeling somewhat disgruntled. I'd only been trying to do what I'd promised to do. That is, give support. And how could Mum say it was just between her and Priya? It was my baby as well, wasn't it? My collection of cells too.

'Honestly,' said Priya, 'this isn't a snap decision. I've done a lot of thinking about it. I've worked out where I stand. I don't want my life ruined and I don't see why it should be. I know we made a mistake and you have to pay for your mistakes, but I've been paying! We've both been paying. Believe me! We have. But I don't think what we did was so terrible that we deserve to go on paying for the rest of our lives.'

'It's not what you did that was terrible,' said Mum. 'It's what you're proposing to do. And while we're on the subject of rights, *your* rights, I'd like to ask you: what about mine? Don't I have any? In case it may have escaped your notice, that is my grandchild you're carrying. I don't suppose you've thought of that?'

Priya bit her lip.

'It's not only *my* grandchild, it's your mum and dad's grandchild. And they don't even know it exists! What about their right?'

'Mum!' I almost screamed it at her.

'Sam, will you please keep out of this?' said Mum

'No, I won't!' I thumped angrily on the arm of the sofa. 'This is my future that you're talking about here just as much as anyone else's!'

'Keep your voice down,' said Mum. 'Your dad will hear us.'

'"Your dad will hear us!" Oh, my goodness, we

can't have that,' I said, 'can we? We can't have Dad disturbed. We're sitting here talking about life and death, but whatever we do we mustn't disturb Dad!'

'Do you mind?' said Mum. 'Priya and I have managed so far to have a perfectly civilised discussion without any need for shouting or recrimination. That sort of thing does nothing to help. Now, Priya, listen to me. I have a suggestion to make. You go home and you tell your mum and dad. Be brave! It has to be done. Admit that you came to me first because you didn't want to upset them. Tell them you've decided to have the baby, and if you don't feel you can keep it – if they don't feel they can keep it...well!' said Mum, going a bit pink. 'I'd be quite happy to take it for you.'

What? I gaped at her. Was Mum out of her mind? A *baby?*

'I've already brought up four,' said Mum. 'I could easily bring up another. Though I daresay,' she added, 'once it's arrived your mum and dad will love it too much to part with it. They'll want to keep it for themselves.'

Priya stood up. 'I couldn't possibly ask that of them. They work far too hard. But thank you for your advice, Mrs Virgo. I really appreciate your not being angry with us. And for the meal! It was lovely. And now I – I think I ought to go, please, Sam.'

'Sure!' I leapt to my feet. 'I'll see you home.'

'Think about what I said,' urged Mum.

'I will,' said Priya.

I knew that she wouldn't. I'm not sure that Mum did.

Chapter Nine

Priya and I walked to the bus-stop in silence. A bus came almost immediately. We got on it, still in silence. The top deck was empty. We sat at the front, staring miserably out of the window.

'I wasn't any help, was it?' I said.

What had I expected? That we'd manage to talk Mum round? That somehow, amazingly, she'd come up with the money for an abortion?

'She meant well,' I said. 'It's just...she's a bit old-fashioned in her views.'

'It's not old-fashioned,' said Priya. 'Lots of people think like that. My mum probably does.'

'You reckon, if you told her, she'd make you have it?'

Priya turned on me, fiercely. 'No one can *make* me have it.'

'Sorry! Sorry!' I backed off, holding my hands up as a sign of peace. 'What I meant...she'd *want* you to have it.'

'Hardly that,' muttered Priya.

'But she wouldn't go for the idea of abortion?'

Priya shrugged. 'Don't know. Never asked her.'

'You don't think —'

'What?' she glared at me. 'What don't I think?'

Timidly, I said, 'You don't think you should do like Mum said?'

'No.'

Just that one word: *no.* Talking to Mum had put Priya in a really combative mood. She was fighting mad, ready to take on all comers.

'See, I just don't know what else we're going to do.' I said it as apologetically as I could. I mean, I felt rough about it. I felt terrible. But I'd just run clean out of ideas.

'I told you,' said Priya. 'I'd sooner kill myself.'

'Right! OK! So that means you're depressed. That means you've got a good case for going to your doctor and—'

'No.'

Again, the brick wall. We came up against it every time. Exasperated, I said, 'So what do you suggest?'

'I'll find a way! I'll go horse riding. I'll have hot baths. I'll stick a knit—'

'Don't be bloody stupid!' I snarled it at her.

'Do you want to end up dead?'

'I just said, didn't I? Anything rather than this!'

'Priya, please! Pull yourself together,' I said. 'Getting hysterical doesn't help. We're in this mess and we might just as well face up to it.'

'*We're* in this mess? *We're* in it?' She yelled it at me. Priya, who never yells. Priya, who is so soft-spoken. 'You're not the one that's got something growing inside you! You're just the one that put it there!'

'Priya!' I caught hold of her. She struggled, but I held on tight. 'Stop this! *Please.* Calm down!'

'How can I calm down? Every day it's getting bigger. You've no idea what it's like! Your mum and her *homilies.*'

She's always using these words that I don't understand. Sometimes they're words I've never heard of.

'It's not her body, is it? So what right's she got? What right's she got to tell me what to do with my own body?' The tears were pouring down Priya's cheeks as she spoke. 'I don't want this thing inside me! I don't want it! I don't want it!'

Suddenly she was crumpled against me, her head on my shoulder, shaking with sobs. That was the moment a couple of people chose to come up the stairs. It would be, wouldn't it?

'Priya, listen!' I whispered it, urgently. I still held her crushed in my arms. 'I know this whole thing is ghastly, and I know it's my fault and that I'm the one that should have found a way out, and I haven't, but all I can say is that I'm here for you, I'll always be here for you, no matter what, as long as you want me, I'll be with you. I promise! I give you my solemn word! I swear!'

I felt a shiver run through her. I tipped her face up, so that she was forced to look at me.

'Did you hear what I said? *Whatever happens*, we'll be together. You and me. For always. Yes?'

'Yes.'

'It's not like you'll be on your own. I'll never let that happen!'

'No.'

She was agreeing with me, meekly, obediently, like a child. Or maybe she was just humouring me. Just trying to make me feel better. I wasn't sure that my words were having any real impact. But it was the best I could do! What else could I do?

We got off the bus and walked in silence along

the High Street. Anxiously, Priya said, 'I don't look as if I've been crying, do I?'

'You look fine.'

Secretly I couldn't help feeling it would have been better if she *had* looked as if she'd been crying. Then maybe her mum would have noticed and asked her what was wrong, and maybe at last Priya would have plucked up the courage to tell her. I don't very often agree with Mum but I did think that Priya ought to confide in her parents. I thought Mum was right and they wouldn't be anywhere near as upset as she seemed to imagine. Of course they wouldn't be pleased; no parent would be pleased. But at the end of the day, as Mum had said, having a baby was perfectly natural. And if Mum was really willing to look after it...

That was an odd thing! That was a very odd thing. Mum, with Priya's baby? Well, my baby, too. But Mum? At her age?

I put it to the back of my mind, to be thought about later. For the moment, my concern was all for Priya.

'Don't do anything stupid,' I begged. 'Please, Priya! You've got to promise me!'

'Sam,' she cried, 'what *could* I do? If I could see

any way out, I would take it!'

Mum pounced the minute I got in. She must have been sitting with her ears on stalks, waiting for the front gate to go.

'Sam!' She beckoned me, furtively, to follow her into the kitchen. (Why furtive? Was she scared Dad would come poking out? But Dad couldn't have cared less.) 'Out here! Let's talk.'

What was there to talk about? We'd said everything there was to say – unless I could persuade her into changing her mind, and I just had this feeling that any attempt would be worse than futile. Mum can be really stubborn. She digs her toes in and there's no budging her.

'Sit down. I'll make a cup of tea.'

Oh, Mum, please! Not a rerun of yesterday. I don't think I could bear it.

I said, 'Mum, I've got homework to do.'

'Not at this time of night. Don't be silly.'

'My maths,' I bleated; but Mum ignored me.

'Priya seems like a nice young girl,' she said. And then immediately went and blew it by adding, 'In spite of everything.'

I felt myself begin to bristle. A bad start, Mum! A really bad start.

'How long did you say you'd known her?'

'About...eighteen months.'

'And in all that time you've never mentioned her! You've never brought her home.'

Statement of fact. It didn't seem to call for an answer, so I didn't offer one.

'I'd have thought you would have done, if she was so important to you.'

Mum turned, the kettle in her hand. 'Why didn't you, Sam? Why didn't you ever bring her?'

'I – don't really know. I guess we...always had other things to do.'

'Have you been back to her place?'

'Um – yeah. Once or twice.'

'You've met her mum and dad?'

'Mm.'

I really hoped Mum would leave it there, but no, she had to keep at it. It was obviously something that rankled. She'd obviously been turning it over in her mind while I was taking Priya home.

'I suppose the reason you never brought her back is the same reason you never want me to attend any of your school functions.'

'You could attend school functions!'

'I *could.* I know that. But I've never been invited, have I?'

'Didn't think you'd be interested,' I mumbled.

'Since when have I ever not shown an interest in what you're up to? Of course I'd be interested. I just didn't want to embarrass you.'

I squirmed. 'Why should you embarrass me?'

'Oh, come on, Sam! I'm not stupid. I know you're ashamed of me.'

I protested that this simply wasn't true; but even as I said it I could feel my cheeks grow hot.

'There, you see! You're blushing. You can't hide things from me. I was watching you the other day, when we saw that film.'

'What film?' I said, though I knew which one she was talking about.

'That *Grape* thing.'

Gilbert Grape. Johnny Depp in the name part. I really like Johnny Depp. I guess he kind of reminds me of me. At least, he did in that film. I really identified with him in that film.

Anyway. In case you haven't seen it, its full title is *What's Eating Gilbert Grape?* It's about this boy, Gilbert, that has a huge fat mother. And when I say fat, I mean FAT. Far fatter than Mum. Mum is gross, but Gilbert's mum is grotesque. Leastways, that's what you start off thinking. By the end of the film you're beginning to feel sorry for her. You're beginning to see her as a real person rather than just this mound of flesh. But the thing is, the point of the film, old Gilbert, he's dead embarrassed by her. He loves her, just like I love Mum; but little snotty-nosed kids come jumping up at the windows, trying to catch a glimpse of the fat lady, and that really gets to him. That really makes him cringe.

I knew how he felt.

'It's all right,' said Mum. 'You don't have to say anything. I'm not surprised you're ashamed of me. Big fat woman, wobbling about. But I wasn't always like this, you know! It's what comes of having four babies.'

I felt a sudden surge of anger. *Babies.* We were back to *babies.* Did she think of nothing else?

'You didn't have to have four! Four is obscene!'

'I suppose you'd rather I got rid of you.'

I could hardly say she shouldn't have got pregnant in the first place. I was hardly in a position to say that. (It's really weird, trying to imagine her and Dad going at it. Well, Dad at any rate.)

'Just think on,' said Mum. 'If I'd been of the

same turn of mind as your girlfriend, you wouldn't be here!'

'What you've never known, you don't miss,' I said.

'Sam Virgo, I gave you the gift of life, and you dare to throw it back in my face!'

'I'm not throwing it back in your face, but you didn't do it for me! You did it for *you.* I didn't ask to be born! And I don't see you had any right to preach at Priya. She was already upset enough without that. You just went and made it worse!'

'Well, thank you. Thank you very much,' said Mum. 'And there was I, thinking that in the circumstances I was being more than generous. There aren't many mums would offer house room to their son's illegitimate offspring, I can tell you!'

'Oh, so it's my illegitimate offspring now,' I said. 'When you were going on at Priya about murdering it, it was your grandchild!'

Mum's face grew sort of mottled. I could see I'd really riled her.

'That's unworthy. You ought to be ashamed of yourself! I made that offer out of the goodness of my heart.'

'No, you didn't,' I said. 'You're just high on babies!'

I found it hard to get to sleep that night. I lay awake for hours, tossing and turning, thinking of Priya, thinking of Mum. I'd gone and hurt both of them. I loved my mum; I really did. So, all right, she was fat. Nobody was ever going to look at her and go, 'Wow! Sam Virgo's mum's a bit of all right!' People were always going to stare. In the street, on the bus. Covertly, pretending not to. I knew they did it; I'd watched them at it.

So what? She was my mum, she'd brought me into the world, she'd loved me and cared for me...what did it matter what she looked like?

I don't know; but it did. I knew that it shouldn't. I knew what Priya would say.

'People are people, Sam! Physical appearance is only external. It's not that important.'

But it reflected on *me*, didn't it? This was my mum, and it really bothered me.

Priya didn't have my uncertainties. She knew who she was, she knew where she was going. At least, she had before I came into her life and messed it up.

God! Oh, God! What were we going to do? I

couldn't be a father! Priya couldn't be a mother! This whole thing was like a nightmare. One unguarded moment, and the whole world had come crashing about our ears. We didn't deserve this! We hadn't done anything wrong! Only loved each other.

When finally I fell asleep it was to the sound of Priya's despairing cry, echoing through my head:

'If I could see any way out, I would take it!'

Chapter Ten

At some stage during that restless night I came to a decision. It was the only one I could think of. Somehow, between us, Priya and me were just going to have to save up the money that we needed.

I didn't know how late you could leave these things, but it seemed to me we'd caught it in time. I mean, it wasn't like Priya had just let it go on, like some girls do. I'd read where some girls, nobody ever knew they were pregnant until they actually had the baby. I'd read where some girls never even knew themselves. I don't know how this could happen. I guess they'd have had to be on the fat side to begin with. You'd know with Priya, all right. But I reckoned we could save up enough to get it done before anyone grew suspicious – well, if Mum didn't spill the beans, that is. I went cold all over at the thought of her going to Priya's mum and dad.

But somehow I didn't think she would. I just couldn't see her doing it. I reckoned what Mum would do, she'd keep *stumm* in the hope we'd leave it too late so that in the end Priya would be forced into having the baby whether she liked it or not. Only that wasn't going to happen! Not if I had anything to do with it.

We only earned a stingy thirty pounds a day from Parkin's and we'd obviously need to keep a bit back for ordinary living, but even so, we ought to be able to manage, say, fifty a week between us. That would soon mount up.

I tried working it out in my head. We'd already got thirty, plus what we'd earned on Saturday, which would bring it up to, say, eighty. That left two hundred, or two-twenty if we couldn't manage it in under fourteen weeks, which we probably couldn't 'cos that would only give us another three weeks to do it in.

OK. So fifty into two hundred and twenty went, say, five times. Five plus eleven is sixteen. Sixteen weeks! That wasn't too late, was it?

No! It couldn't be. She'd have told me if it was. The woman at the clinic. She'd have said. 'Don't leave it longer than fourteen weeks.'

I reckoned sixteen would be just about OK.

I went down to breakfast feeling pretty pleased with myself. I'd solved all our problems! I'd ring Priya that morning and tell her. That would cheer her up!

'I can't imagine what you're looking so happy for,' said Mum. 'In the circumstances.'

'It's being so cheerful keeps me going,' I said.

'I wouldn't be so sure about that. Your dad wants a word with you.'

'About what?'

'What do you think?'

The baby? But I'd already been through all that with Mum! Anyway, it wasn't a baby. It was a foetus. A collection of cells. And nobody was going to change our minds. We were going to have an abortion and we were going to pay for it ourselves. It was our money: it was our right.

I sat myself down at the breakfast table, prepared to do battle. And then Dad came in. And that was when he dropped it on me.

'That new window,' he said. 'It's going to cost the better part of two hundred pounds.'

'You what?' I said.

'Better part two hundred pounds.'

'Two hundred *pounds*? That's outrageous! You're being done!'

I realise now it was an unfortunate choice of words. At the time, it didn't occur to me. Not until Dad, rather dryly, said, 'That's a bit rich, coming from where it does.'

I felt my cheeks grow hot.

'I was going to pay you back!'

'You are going to pay me back.'

What was that supposed to mean? I hadn't taken anything!

'I could do the job for half the money,' I said. 'I mean...what are you paying for? Gold-plated locks?'

'I'm not paying for anything,' said Dad. 'You are.'

'Me?' I stared at him, aghast.

'You broke it, you pay for it.'

' But – you were going to have a new one, anyway! You said! It was rotten!'

'I wouldn't have had an emergency call-out fee, just to board it up.'

'I could have boarded it up!'

'First thing Saturday morning? I doubt it.'

'Well, all right! I'll pay the call-out fee.'

'You'll pay the lot. I shall expect it at the rate of twenty pounds a week.'

'But that'll take for ever!'

'So be it.' Dad reached out a scrawny arm for the toast. 'I won't charge you interest.'

'Mum!' I appealed to her, across the table. 'It's not right I should have to pay for something that was going to have to be done anyway!'

'I think it's very right, Sam. I think your dad's being more than fair. After all, he could have gone to the police.'

Shopped his own son? I didn't actually say it, but Mum obviously guessed that's what I was thinking.

'You being his son just makes it all the worse. You can't do a thing like that and expect to get away scot free. Everything has its price.'

And the price in this case was two-thirds of my earnings for the next ten weeks... How could I save enough to help Priya with that kind of extortion going on? It was sheer daylight robbery! That anyone could have the brass face to charge two hundred pounds for making one small window frame! What were they using, for God's sake? *Mahogany?* I could have done it myself, quite easily, if he'd just thought to ask me.

I'm good at that kind of thing.

And I'd probably have made a better job of it.

They just wanted me to suffer, that was what it was. Vengeance is mine. *You are being punished.*

They knew what I'd wanted that money for. They knew I was desperate.

I sat through breakfast in sour silence while Dad ate his toast and read the newspaper and Mum wittered on in her usual inconsequential fashion. Something about teabags. Something to do with trying a new brand because the last lot had kept bursting in the water. I didn't bother listening. I was feeling too sore.

As I pushed back my chair Mum said, 'Did Priya tell her parents yet?'

'How would I know?' I said. Rudely; I admit it. But they'd just punched me in the guts. 'I haven't had a chance to talk to her since last night, have I?'

'Well, when you next speak,' said Mum, 'you just make sure that she intends to do it.'

'I can't *make* Priya do *anything*,' I said.

I wouldn't mind betting it was Mum had egged Dad on. Urged him to cripple me; charge me full whack. Anything to stop me helping Priya!

I went upstairs to my room and kicked savagely at the skirting board. Then I saw my football and started slamming it about. Wham! Bam! *And the ball bounces off the bed leg and into the wardrobe...and it's a goal! It's a goal!*

Mum's voice came up the stairwell. 'Sam! What are you doing? Stop it, you'll have the ceiling down.'

And then I suppose I'd have to pay for that, as well. I sank down on to the bed, the football between my knees. There had to be a way...I couldn't just give up!

Maybe I could sell things?

I let my gaze move slowly round the room, searching for anything I could possibly offload without Mum immediately noticing. It was pathetic how little stuff I had. I mean, real stuff. I had junk, all right. I had junk by the barrowload. But anything of real value, forget it!

Old clapped-out radio. That could go. And my Walkman. And my CDs. I might be able to get something for those. Maybe a few of my clothes, ones that Mum might have forgotten about or wouldn't discover until it was too late.

Computer games. Old wind-up watch, dating

from the Stone Age. Football; I guess someone might give a few bob for a football. Maybe. I dunno, it's a bit tatty. *But what else is there?*

I'd willingly have flogged both my computer and my CD player to get Priya out of the mess I'd got her into, except that the computer had been new for my birthday and the CD player was a Christmas present and Mum's eagle eyes would spot their absence immediately.

Well, and so what? So Mum would notice they'd gone. *Who cared?*

Mentally, I added the computer and the CD player to my list.

Next I sat down and itemised everything. All the stuff I could sell and how much I reckoned I could get for it if I advertised it on one of the school boards. Altogether it came to a hundred and twenty-five pounds. A paltry sum, but I knew there wasn't any point pitching the prices too high. No one's exactly flush, at our dump.

I did a print-out on the computer, to take in to school with me next day to show Priya. I wanted her to see that it was a good plan: a plan that would work. We could still manage to get the money! And I would pay her back every penny, just as soon as

I'd finished paying Dad. I would! Every single penny.

Stoo called round in the middle of the morning and they all went into the garden to drink coffee, so I took the opportunity to call Priya and tell her my plan, except she wasn't there. I'd forgotten, they were all going off to spend the day with Auntie Sheela (the one who disapproved of the way she and Yogesh had been brought up). I left a message on the answerphone. I said, 'This is a message for Priya. Priya, this is Sam. I just wanted you to know that I'm working on something. It's going to be OK. I'll tell you about it tomorrow.'

I didn't want to put her on the spot. I thought if one of her parents asked her what it meant, she could always say it was a project for school. But I didn't think they would. Priya's mum and dad weren't like mine. They both took an interest, but they never meddled. If anyone left a message for me on an answerphone (if we had an answerphone, which we don't) Mum would instantly demand to know who it was and what it was all about. (She just can't resist questions.)

* * *

Monday was the day of our visit to the British Museum. We were going by train, about twenty of us in all. I still hadn't handed in my permission form, but I just tagged on anyway. Mrs Huxtable was in charge and she lives on a different planet. She's OK with Egyptian mummies and ancient sarcophaguses, but she's not really part of the ordinary world. She looked at her list and said worriedly, 'I don't seem to have your name down here, Sam.'

'You should have,' I said. 'I got my form signed.'

'Then why isn't your name here?'

'I dunno. I guess someone forgot to write it down.'

'You mean, I forgot to write it down.' She has this reputation for forgetting things. 'Oh, well.' She gave a resigned sigh and took out her pen. 'I suppose it will be all right. Now that you're here.'

'I'd be dead disappointed,' I said.

'Yes, I'm sure. Go on! Get in line.'

The time we were travelling, the train was pretty empty.

'Keep together,' said Mrs Huxtable. 'All in the same carriage.'

I took Priya's hand and tugged her further

along, up the corridor, until we found one of those little itty-bitty compartments all on their own.

'OK. Now. Hear this! This is the plan.'

I told her how I'd come to a decision: if nobody would help us, we'd just have to help ourselves.

'I got you into this mess, I'll get you out of it!'

I explained how I'd got to pay my dad two hundred pounds for his rotten window but how, if I sold a load of stuff, I'd be able to contribute something straightaway and would make up the rest later.

'Rest of what?' said Priya.

'Of the money! For the clinic! All it means is you saving something out of your Saturday money. You could do that, couldn't you?'

Priya nodded.

'I'll pay you back,' I told her. 'Just as soon as I've paid Dad. I reckon it'll take about six or seven weeks.'

'To pay your dad?'

'No!' Either I wasn't explaining myself properly or Priya just wasn't with it. It's unusual for her. She's usually very quick on the uptake. 'To save up the money. Six or seven weeks, then we'll have enough. Well, say, eight at the very most. But that'd still be all right. It wouldn't be too late. See?' I gave her a squeeze. 'I told you I'd find a way!'

I waited for her to say something. Something on the lines of, 'Oh, Sam! I knew you wouldn't let me down.' But she didn't. She didn't say anything. Just sat there, frozen, like a statue.

'You'd still only be sixteen weeks,' I urged.

'Seventeen,' said Priya.

'Well...seventeen. Maybe. At the worst. But that's OK, isn't it?'

'I s'pose so.'

'That's not too late!'

Priya hunched a shoulder.

'I mean, I didn't actually ask the latest they could do it, but—'

'Twenty-four weeks,' said Priya. She said it kind of...blankly. Without any expression.

'Twenty-four!' I gave her another squeeze. 'Well, then! We've got bags of time!'

'Bags,' said Priya.

'I know it seems like for ever,' I said, 'but we can still get it done before Christmas. Well before Christmas! And I don't think anyone would notice anything. Not at that stage. Would they?'

'Dunno,' said Priya.

'I don't think so,' I said.

I was trying to jolly her along. Rouse a bit of enthusiasm. Well, not enthusiasm, perhaps. That's not quite the word. Trying to get a bit of a reaction. Something a bit more positive. I mean, here I was, putting the solution to our problem, and she was just sitting there, in a heap, like she'd lost all interest. I hadn't expected her to be *grateful*. But I had expected something.

'Priya?' I said. 'Are you all right?'

Tonelessly, she said, 'I was sick this morning.'

'Sick?'

'Sick.'

I didn't know what to say. 'Badly?'

'Mm.'

I put my arm round her. 'It won't go on for ever!'

'My mum will find out. I can't keep it from her. Our bathroom...you can hear everything!'

I pulled her closer.

'Look, if you think eight weeks is too long I could always ring up somewhere else ... see if we could get it done right away and pay in instalments. I mean, you never know! If we explained...they might let us.'

'Die now, pay later.'

'Nobody's going to die!'

'*It* is.'

'Priya! It's only a collection of cells,' I said. 'Don't start personalising.'

'I'm not. But we're still planning to kill it. Whatever it is.'

'Well...we don't *have* to,' I said. 'If you've changed your mind.'

'I haven't changed my mind!' She snatched at the sheet of paper I was holding. 'What's this? What are all these figures?'

'That's how we're going to get the money. See?' I pointed, glad to have something concrete to talk about. 'Those are the things I thought I could sell.'

'Your CDs? Oh, Sam! You can't sell your CDs!'

'Why not? They're only things. I can always buy them again later.'

'But they're all your favourites!'

A tear trickled slowly down her cheek and plopped on to the collar of her blouse.

'Oh, Priya, listen! Cheer up! We're *doing* something,' I said. 'We've taken the first step... everything's going to be all right!'

I really believed that. I really believed we'd got the thing cracked.

We lingered behind the others as we walked across Victoria Station to the underground. Was Priya really a bit shaky, a bit unsteady, or am I only imagining it? No, I think she must have been, because I remember putting an arm about her shoulders and I remember a tremor running through her.

'Priya! It's going to be *all right*,' I whispered.

Mrs Huxtable turned, as we reached the ticket barrier. She beckoned, impatiently. 'Come along, you two! All keep together.'

We took our time. We weren't in a hurry. We got to the top of the escalator, that long escalator going down to the Victoria tube line, as the last of the others were stepping off at the bottom.

'Sam Virgo and Priya Patel!' yelled Mrs Huxtable. 'What are you doing? Get a move on!'

'Daft old bat,' I muttered.

Priya shook her head. She seemed...very far away, somehow.

'She's only doing her job,' she said. 'She's responsible if anything happens.'

'*She's* not responsible for you,' I told her. 'I am!'

'Oh, Sam.' I remember she smiled at me. I remember that smile. It haunts me even now.

I don't know how to describe it. I don't have the words! It was just so...*sorrowful.*

'Sam Virgo!' That was Mrs Huxtable, bawling at us again. 'What's the hold up?'

'Keep your hair on,' I said. 'We're coming.'

We took the first step, together, on to the escalator. And that was when it happened.

I thought I had hold of Priya's hand. I really did. But our grasp must have been broken as she fell. I watched, helpless with horror, as her body went hurtling downwards. Someone shrieked. It may have been Mrs Huxtable. It may have been one of the girls. I don't know.

We never got to the British Museum.

Chapter Eleven

Priya lost the baby. I guess falling headfirst down a moving staircase is a pretty effective way of giving yourself an abortion. But I wouldn't recommend it. I really wouldn't.

Not that she did it intentionally. I mean, just in case anyone's thinking that she might have done, I am here to state, categorically, that she most certainly did not. She told me this when I went to visit her in the hospital. She seemed really anxious that I should know.

'I didn't do it on purpose, Sam! You've got to believe me!'

'I believe you,' I said. I would always believe anything Priya told me.

'Do you honestly?' She clutched at my hand. 'Do you, Sam?'

'You know I do!'

'People don't fall down escalators on purpose.

They don't! You couldn't!'

'Of course you couldn't. You just caught your foot, that was all. It was an accident.'

I didn't see why it should bother her so much. After all, no one was accusing her. But she kept returning to it.

'I never meant it to happen, Sam! Not that way! I know we were planning to – get rid of it, but…I didn't do it on purpose!'

It made me uncomfortable, the way she kept saying that. I muttered that she oughtn't be dwelling on it. I was worried she was upsetting herself. I thought they might stop me seeing her – they might think I was responsible.

'It's over, it's finished! We can get back to normal.'

'I don't feel normal!'

'You will,' I promised. 'Just as soon as you get out of here. When do you think they'll let you?'

'I – don't know. Soon. Maybe. Sam!' Her fingers tightened their grip. 'Sam, I keep thinking!'

'Thinking what?'

'Suppose I really did?'

I said, *'Did?'*

'Do it on purpose!'

'Well, but you didn't. You've just told me.' I put my other hand over hers and gave it a squeeze. 'Nobody does a thing like that on purpose. It's not something that people do. They do other things – terrible things. But they don't do that. Least, I've never heard of anyone doing that.'

'They throw themselves under trains,' said Priya.

There was a silence. I racked my brain for a way to change the subject.

'Did I tell you about Baz?' I said. 'He—'

'I thought of throwing myself under a train,' said Priya.

'Priya, please!' I said. 'Don't!'

'I'm just telling you. I did.'

'When did you?'

'After I spoke with your mum.'

'You didn't mean it,' I said. 'You wouldn't actually have done it.'

She turned her face up towards me. Her eyes, dark and deeply troubled, looked searchingly into mine.

'How do we know?' she whispered.

'*I* know,' I said, ''cos I know you. I know you wouldn't do something like that. You're not that sort of person. Only selfish people do things like that. In any case,' I said, 'we had a plan, remember?'

'You were going to sell your CDs.'

'That's right!'

'All your favourites.'

'Yes, and now I won't have to. So that's one good thing, isn't it?'

What I was trying to do, I was trying to cheer her up a bit. Make her laugh. Maybe it wasn't too sensitive of me, I dunno. But I reckoned she'd be glad about not being pregnant any more. I mean, it was what she'd wanted. It was what she'd been desperate for. I'd have thought she'd be jumping for joy.

Well, perhaps not quite that. I guess people don't actually *jump for joy* when they've managed to rid themselves totally accidentally of a baby they never wanted in the first place. I guess that might be sort of crude. Even if it was only a collection of cells. But surely she'd got to be feeling at least a little bit relieved?

Well, that's what I'd have thought. I mean, I was! Feeling relieved, I mean. Once I knew Priya was going to be OK, I just felt that a huge great weight had been lifted from my shoulders. Why didn't she?

It just goes to show what I've always suspected, that I don't really know too much about the female sex. It must be something to do with hormones. I mean, it is totally *illogical.*

'Priya, please!' I begged. 'Please don't cry! They'll think I'm upsetting you. I can still sell my CDs if it'll make you feel better. I could give the money to Oxfam. Or starving children. Anything! A sort of penance.'

That made her laugh. Or at any rate smile. I knew I'd get there in the end.

'Penance for what?' she said.

I handed her a couple of paper hankies.

'For being bad. Giving you a rough time.'

'Oh, Sam!' said Priya. 'I do love you!'

Before I was even allowed to go and visit Priya in hospital I had to go round and see her mum and dad. They wanted to talk to me. That was bad, that was. I felt like some kind of...I dunno! Traitor, or something. They'd let me and Priya be together, they'd put their trust in us, and I'd gone and betrayed them.

Priya's dad, especially, he was pretty hopping

mad. He chewed me out good and proper. But then Priya's mum stepped in and said she reckoned he'd said all that needed to be said.

'I think Sam already feels quite guilty enough. And don't let's pretend that Priya had nothing to do with it.'

'It wasn't her fault!' I said.

'I'm not sure she'd go along with that. She's a very strong-minded young woman.' Her mum smiled slightly. 'You may have noticed!'

'Yeah, but...I was the one talked her into it.'

'Precisely!' Priya's dad was on it in a flash. 'If it hadn't been for him—'

'Please.' Mrs Patel held up a hand. 'No more! Go and visit her, Sam. I think it would help her.'

When Priya was let out of hospital she didn't come back to school. Her mum explained to me.

'We're sending her to India for a few months to stay with her grandparents. We feel it would be best. Just so she can get herself sorted. Another thing –' she paused, ' – could we ask you, Sam, to make us one promise?'

I nodded. What else could I do?

'Could we ask you, please, not to write to Priya for at least three months?'

My face must have fallen because she added, quickly, that it wasn't supposed to be a punishment.

'We're not sending her in to exile. We're not trying to separate her from you. We just feel that she's been under a lot of pressure and it would be helpful if she could get away for a bit. We think perhaps we tend to push her rather too hard. She takes life very seriously, you know, Sam. In many ways, you've actually been very good for her.'

I grew a bit hot when she said that.

'Yes, I know,' she said. 'I know! You've both behaved foolishly, but I'm sure you've learnt your lesson. I'm not going to lecture you. We've been through all that. I could wish you hadn't done what you did, but I think one has to keep it in perspective. When all's said and done, there are far worse things going on in the world.'

'You haven't told Auntie Sheela,' I said, 'have you?'

Priya's mum gave a great peal of laughter. 'That's exactly what Priya said!'

'She's really scared of Auntie Sheela. She reckons she'd say you've brought her up badly.'

'Oh, she says that anyway! We're all quite used to

Auntie Sheela. But no, rest assured! We haven't told her. It shall be our little secret.'

Priya's mum is really ace.

I've got to say it, my mum isn't so bad. I know I go on about her, but basically she's sound. She was really sympathetic when she heard about Priya. She sent her a get-well card and she warned me, before I went to visit, to be gentle with her.

'She'll still be feeling fragile, Sam.'

I thought that was a bit unnecessary, to tell you the truth. I mean, what else would I be but gentle? It was only when I got there and Priya started crying that I thought maybe Mum knew what she was talking about.

She asked me, when I got back, 'How is she coping?'

'She keeps dwelling on things.' I told her how Priya kept repeating, over and over, that she didn't do it on purpose, and how the least little thing seemed to set her off crying. I don't know why I told Mum; I guess I just felt the need to talk.

'It's like she's feeling guilty about it,' I said.

'Well, she most likely would,' agreed Mum. 'It's only natural.'

'But she couldn't help it! It was an accident!'

'Imagine how much worse she'd feel if it hadn't been. If you'd gone ahead with that idea of yours.'

I frowned. I wasn't sure I could let Mum get away with that.

'I don't know that she would have felt worse. After all, that would have been a conscious decision.'

'Don't you kid yourself,' said Mum.

* * *

Priya's back in India now, with her grandparents. And I'm writing it all down. All the things that happened. I guess it's a sort of therapy. Getting it out of my system. Working through the guilt. I dunno! I just somehow felt the need. Partly it's because I miss her so much. I miss her like crazy! I really do. She promised to write to me as soon as the three months was up and I know that she will. Priya always keeps her promises.

I love her so much! I know she once said that you couldn't get married at sixteen because you still had a lot of growing up to do and you might change your mind and not be in love any more, but it's simply not true! However much I change, I shall always love her. I think of her all the time. In class, in bed, on the bus...Saturday mornings. Saturday evenings. Saturday evenings are when I miss her most. They were our time, our special time.

Just occasionally, I even think of the baby. The collection of cells. I look at babies in prams, or at women who are pregnant, and I can't help wondering...what would it have been like?

Guys aren't meant to do that sort of thing. Lee and Baz and the rest, they'd think I'd gone soft. And don't get me wrong. No way did I want to become a dad at sixteen. No way! I agree with Priya absolutely. One hundred per cent. It's a woman's right to choose. It's her body, no one else's. But maybe I have a bit more understanding of Mum's point of view than I had before.

I think perhaps it hit Priya, too, and that was why she kept begging me to reassure her...nobody falls down an escalator on purpose.

One day, maybe, this is something we'll discuss.

I hope she writes to me soon! I need to know that she still loves me.

I'm sure she does. She told me she did, the night before she left.

'I love you, Sam...now and for ever.'

The three months is up on Monday. That's just four days away. It would take four days, I should think, for a letter to reach her. That means I could write! I could write this very minute! From this point on, I can write whenever I want!

Except that now I've picked up my pen I can't really think what to say. Just that *I love you…*

I LOVE YOU I LOVE
YOU I LOVE YOU I
LOVE YOU I LOVE
YOU I LOVE YOU I
LOVE YOU I LOVE
YOU XXX SAM

More Orchard Black Apples

Title	Author	ISBN
Love is for Ever	*Jean Ure*	978 1 84616 959 5 *
Get a Life	*Jean Ure*	978 1 84121 831 1
Ella Mental and the Good Sense Guide	*Amber Deckers*	978 1 84362 727 2
Ella Mental – Life, Love and More Good Sense	*Amber Deckers*	978 1 84616 212 1
Deeper Than Blue	*Jill Hucklesby*	978 1 84616 342 5
Last Kiss of the Butterfly	*Jill Hucklesby*	978 1 84616 343 2
Hazel, Not a Nut	*Gill Lobel*	978 1 84362 448 6
Stargirl	*Jerry Spinelli*	978 1 84616 599 3
Eggs	*Jerry Spinelli*	978 1 84616 700 3
Milkweed	*Jerry Spinelli*	978 1 84362 485 1

All priced at £4.99, apart from those marked * which are £5.99.
Orchard Red Apples are available from all good bookshops,
or can be ordered direct from the publisher:
Orchard Books, PO BOX 29, Douglas IM99 1BQ
Credit card orders please telephone 01624 836000
or fax 01624 837033
or e-mail: bookshop@enterprise.net for details.

To order please quote title, author and ISBN
and your full name and address.
Cheques and postal orders should be made payable to 'Bookpost plc.'
Postage and packing is FREE within the UK
(overseas customers should add £1.00 per book).

Prices and availability are subject to change.